Star

JUST A CHICKEN
JUST A GIRL

Molly Cox

This is a work of fiction. Names, characters, places, and incidents are probably the author's imagination, but if not, congratulations, you're in a book. Don't be offended. It's really a compliment. For legal reasons, yes I am joking.

First paperback edition July 2021

Book design by Molly Cox and Heath Cox
Illustrations by Molly Cox

ISBN 978-0-578-92941-5 (paperback)

Table of Contents

Note from the Author

"I'm trying to finish my book." I'll say casually.

"You write books?!"

"Well, yeah. I'm working on one."

"Well what's it about?" Eager friends and family ask me.

"It's, um, its about a chicken."

And everyone laughs. It's pretty obvious if you pay attention that I'm obsessed with chickens. But still people are surprised. But, when I finally released my precious papers into beta readers' hands, they laughed in a different way.

"This isn't just a story about a chicken," they say, "it's about Andrea."

And I guess they're right. It's not just about a chicken, which in their defense chickens are super personable and amazing and get a bad rap even though they aren't dumb even a little bit, so there's that. But really, it is a story about family, about friendship, about forgiveness, healing, courage, hope and especially love. And, of course, chickens.

And this story is not just fantasy. Take any time to do any research, and you will find that there are many stories of ducks, geese and chickens who have been beneficial to kids and adults, with a range of needs, addictions to disabilities, and especially, autism. So maybe its a little fantasized, exaggerated for sure, but its not made up. The story was already there, in so many people's lives. I just happened to find it and decide to be the one to give it a voice.

So now I just hope you will listen.

And listen carefully. To Andrea, each word would take a great effort to say and to say what she really means. So don't read fast. Read and think. Pay attention, because life is too fast to read a book that fast as well. And maybe we'd all be a little better off if we just really, truly listened.

-Molly

Star
Chapter 1
A Lifetime Begun: 216

"I peaked out the opening to my drawer-like cage, ignoring the other chicks' chorus blaring from all around me for a moment. "Bleep, Bleep" scanner blared as it was swiped over items; parakeets chirped in their cage next to ours, dogs barked from across the store, customers discussed this or that, all above the chirping that surrounded me. And through it all, what I noticed was a young girl, clinging tightly to a man as they walked around the store, a woman following close behind them. The girl's eyes were sparkled with a splashing feeling that seemed all too familiar to me. They darted around the noisy room, as if searching for a place for them to rest. And now, a store clerk was holding a guinea pig out for the family to see. I watched the black animal wiggle around in his hand, it's whiskers quivering nervously. The girl reached out gingerly, barely touched it's fur but then shuddered and retracted her hand. A dog came out next, bouncing playfully and spinning in circles to contain it's own excitement. The girl, however, contested the puppy as well, her body shaking, her face pale and scared.

My attention was drawn away from the outside world as something growled in my stomach. *Food.* My mind echoed quietly. I walked to the chick feed and pecked at it, but only for a few minutes. Before long my eyelids began to droop. I laid down on the wood shavings beneath me and drifted to sleep...

What was that?! I pulled my eyes open, wide awake all too soon and I bolted. There was a giant finger pointing in my face! Oh. I sighed in relief when I had more distance to see It was the girl I'd been watching earlier. Her face was smiling, though her lips were not. Her Mom walked over to see what she was pointing at.

"It is very cute, Andrea, but you know we wouldn't have a place to keep a chicken."

The young girl frowned, keeping her finger there, motioning like she was petting me through the cage. She pointed to a man a few feet away, who had been with her earlier.

Apparently the woman understood what the girl meant. "Mike," She called, "Andrea found something she likes."

"Coming." The tall man walked over, laying a hand on the girl's shoulder. She shied away with a quick movement and the man let his hand drop without a question. "What is it?"

She pointed once again.

"You want a chick?" He sounded puzzled.

She shook her head and pointed at me again.

"You just like that one?" Her mom questioned, the girl nodded, still pointing.

All the while my heart pounded faster and faster. *Me? Why me?*

"Sweetie, it wouldn't stay that little and

fuzzy, it'd be a big bird. And it would be a lot of work to take care of." She continued looking looked at me silently.

"Is that really what you would want?"

She nodded without looking the other way.

Her parents began to discuss it quietly. "What do you think, Honey?" The man questioned simply.

The mom scratched her head. "I don't know. That's a kinda big investment, isn't it? I mean to buy a coop…?"

"There's plenty of wood in the yard. I'll build one, if we want to."

"Do you think she'd really take care of them or would I be cleaning up after them? I mean, she's only ten."

And immediately the girl apparently heard their quiet conversation and stepped back to them, grabbing the woman's arm and shook her head, before pointing to herself.

"Yes, honey, we know you want it, we're discussing it." Her mom said gently.

The girl shook her head again and pointed to herself again.

"She means she will take care of it, Susan," her dad stepped in and the girl apparently agreed. "I think its a good idea. I mean her therapist said an animal is a good idea, and its the only one she's going to like."

The woman put her hand over her eyes, "It's two against one, isn't it?" She threw up her hands and laughed, "Why not? In any case

I have heard that fresh, organic eggs can be very beneficial to kids with autism." She smiled at her daughter, "you've convinced me."

The girl's eyes sparkled all the more as she looked back at me.

Before long, the family came back with the store clerk and a box.

"We've decided on three." The Dad announced. "Which ones do you want, Andrea?" The girl smiled shyly and pointed at her dad.

"Me?" He asked, surprised, then he shrugged. "Alright." And pointed at a white little chick in the cage below me, who was jumping up and down and cheeping excitedly, hopping into the worker's hand as he reached for her.

Next the girl pointed at her mom.

"Oh, okay." She laughed slightly choosing a red and yellow chick from my cage, the whole drawer shaking as it was opened.

"Now, you're next, Sweetheart. Which one do you want?" Her Dad asked.

Perhaps I shouldn't have been so surprised when this girl chose me, questions racing through my head. I couldn't even think one out before I thought of another. I pushed it aside and tried to accept it all. I was bound to be bought eventually, I suppose it may as well be today. But I didn't know this was going to be a different kind of girl, and make me a different kind of bird.

Chapter 2
Family Flocks Together: 216

"Hi! What's your name? Oh yeah, we don't have names! Silly me. I call myself me, since I don't have a name. What do you call yourself? Or do you call yourself you? Or me? That would be weird. I'm so excited!!"

I spun around in the dark and moving box, cocking my head at the obnoxious white chick as words poured out of her beak. "I'm sorry, what did you say?"

"Who, me? Oh, yeah I was saying… umm…I can't remember! I can say something else if you'd like me to! *Woah!!!*" Without warning, we slid across the floor of the dark box. I froze in fear at the sudden movement.

"What *was* that?" I asked, breathing heavily, trying to right myself.

"I don't know! It was kinda fun! Maybe we'll do it again!"

"I hope not." But sure enough, in just a moment we went sliding the other way. I slammed into the red and yellow chick.

She giggled. "Hi. This is quite the ride, isn't it?"

I quickly righted myself, pretending I didn't look ridiculous. "Hi." Then I frowned, adding dryly, "I don't like it."

With a nudge she said, "Cheer up, little sis, we're going home!"

13

"Sis?" I wondered if I'd heard her right.

"Yep! We're sorta like sisters now, aren't we?"

Excitement and fear both splashed in me at the same time. "I...I guess so...I'd-I guess I'd never thought about it like that..."

"Oh, do you mind if I call you that?"

"Go ahead, please, I just, I don't feel like, I mean, maybe it's, you know..."

"Hey, calm down." Her smile was gentle, but her words confident.

"Eh?" I felt kinda bad I was so distracted.

"I mean you're struttering all over."

"Struttering?" I repeated, now just confused.

"Whatever the word is. You seem all worked up. Just calm down. We'll all be fine."

I couldn't think of anything else to say, so I just looked over at the hoppy white chick trying to peak through the holes in the box. This new "sister", however, quickly caught on.

"Is something wrong?" Her voice was soft and quiet.

"Don't worry about me." I shook my head, still looking the other way. The last thing I wanted was someone else to worry.

"You should be excited." Her words somehow snapped me out of my on world. I should be, and I wanted desperately to be, but I just couldn't, and I shook it off.

"I know. It's just...never mind."

"You can tell me."

I looked up into her caring eyes so honest and pure. I really didn't want to keep hiding it all. And you can hardly blame me, being only about a week old. So I told my sister my worries.

"I'm just scared. I'm really scared. That girl, she chose me, and, and why did she choose me? I'm not ready to be a pet. They— one time, a kid dropped me, at the pet store, and…they said that they were worried they had hurt me. Another kid said I was fine, I was just a chick and didn't matter."

I closed my eyes. "That hurt more than the fall. Now I'm scared. I'm scared I'll fall again, but more, I'm scared I'm not good enough." A car honked nearby and I jumped, sitting down on the floor and shaking. "I'm also scared of loud noises."

My sister sat on the ground next to me. "I'm sorry, sis. I really am. But, you will be okay, I know you will, somehow. It's like when we only have so much food, but it's only how much we need, but as soon as we need more it's refilled by the people who take care of us. There must be someone who somehow always takes care of everyone. And you think you need to not be a pet now or ever, but the one who takes care of us knows you need that food right now, even if you didn't need it before." She smiled, lifting my face forcing me to look into her deep brown eyes. "And besides all that, to me, you *do* matter."

A tear dripped down my fluffy face and I

smiled. My heart suddenly felt a little lighter.
"Thank you." I said to her quietly, but the
serene moment ended quickly ended when the
box shifted again and the white chick, "me",
slid into us.

　　"Oh, hi!" She squealed.

　　I laughed, a full, lighthearted laugh.
Maybe this adventure would be fun, especially
with these two as my sisters. Our little family
of a flock together.

　　And yet the dark fear still lurked on the
edges of my mind, resembling the dark box we
rode in. The only way any light shone through
in the holes on the side. And they threatened to
be easily covered and any hope returning. But
it was still a light and still enough just to see. I
closed my eyes, and took a deep breath, hoping
that one day that kind of light would shine into
the darkness of my mind and heart.

Chapter 3
One Little Star: 216

The light poured in, temporarily blinding us as our box was opened and we were taken to our new home. At last, when my eyes adjusted, I saw the girl, Andrea, hovering over me box.

She smiled softly, singing with a small voice, "'This is Home.'" It was the first time I'd heard her voice, and it was a beautiful voice.

Her parents' tall figures also appeared above us, though I had to crane my neck to see. One scooped us the white chick, and the other the red one. Soon, Andrea's hands came, fear stopping my heart as I saw them reach for me. And yet, they were soft and gentle and encompassed my entire body. As she slowly life me, her amber eyes met mine, and my racing heart slowed.

"Don't they need names?" Andrea's mom asked simply.

When Andrea nodded, her mom said, "Well, I think I'll call her…Lacey. Since she's a Golden Laced Wyandotte."

"I like it." Her dad agreed. "I'll call this little silkie Snowflake, since she's all white. What's her name gonna be Andrea?"

She looked at me and her smile grew, brown eyes twinkling with excitement. The whispered sing song voice was for only my ears and hers, "'Shine bright, little Star. Show the world who you are.' -Mackenzie Felix."

She looked up again, her face bright an hopeful, especially compared to my fearful one. "Star."

+++++++++++

The family soon put us in a much larger box. A red light shone down and warmed my chilled feathers, and the strong scent of the fresh wood shavings was familiar, making my mind slow just enough to comprehend it all. Lacey and Snowflake ran around. I thought of joining, but was a bit too overwhelmed at the moment.

"We're home! Oh, this is our new home! Isn't this exciting?!" They chirped as the ran boisterously. I let myself drown out the noise, my thoughts filling the empty spaces.

Finally I found my voice, **"I'm not ready."** I stated, more to myself that anyone else. Snowflake, however, heard, and skidded to a stop beside me, nearly falling over.

"You aren't ready for what?" Her high voice contrasted my confused spirit.

"I don't know. I guess I'm just not ready to be her pet."

"Oh, relax Star." She said.

My eyes widened at her words. **"What did you say?"**

"I said to relax. Weren't you listening?" She giggled at my oblivion.

"I know. But what did you call me?"

"Star. That's your name now, silly.

I don't have to be "me" anymore. I can
be Snowflake! Yippee! I like my name.
Snowflake. SNOWFLAKE! Hello,
my name is Snowflake, what's yours?
My name in Snowflake. Snowflake,
snowflake, sssnnnnooowwwfffflllllaaakkke.
SNOWFLAKE!"

I drowned out my sister's rambling as
I thought about my new person, Andrea.
She said I was her Star. And... and she was
scared. She was...different, somehow. And
for some reason, I thought, she needed me.
And somehow, I also must have needed her.
But fear gripped those all-too-heartwarming
thoughts. *"It's just a chicken. It doesn't matter."*
The taunting voice of memory reminded me. I
was just a chicken. Nothing I ever did would
matter. I wasn't enough to be a Star, whatever
that was. I just...I wasn't. I couldn't let her
trust in me. Somehow, though I'd just met her,
I already loved her, I didn't want to hurt her.
And I couldn't, I wouldn't let her down. But
how? Lacey said that I mattered to her. And
she said she knew that I'd be alright. But what
if the food ran out and I still needed it, and no
one was there to refill it? I wasn't sure if it was
all true. But right now, I had nothing else to
believe.

Unlike Snowflake, I had to be more "me"
than I'd ever been before. I had to learn who I
was and who I could be. Except I wasn't going
to be called "me". I was going to be called Star.

Chapter 4
The Mirror In Her Eyes: 217

We stayed in the box the first day; something about letting us rest before holding us the next day. I spent the time getting to know my new 'sisters'. To be truthful, we ate and slept most of the day away. No, that's not entirely true. I spent a lot of that time battling with myself.

"Lacey," I finally turned to the red Wyandotte, already learning to lean on her. **"What's a star?"**

Her giggle rang like a sweet bell, **"That's your name, silly."**

"Yeah, I know, but Andrea said that I am her bright star. I don't know what a star is."

Lacey cocked her head. **"Hmm. I'm not sure I do, either. I've never seen a star, I don't think."**

I turned, dejected and no less confused. **"Okay, thanks anyway."**

"No problem."

I stayed there, silent for a moment, I guess hoping that she'd say something else. **"But,"** She somehow read my mind, **"I think stars are good things. Besides, Andrea loves you no matter what you are."**

"But...I can't..."

She laid her wing over me. **"I thinks that the only one telling you that you can't is** yourself. The only one making you afraid is yourself. We're all here for you, but you're the only one who can change yourself."

"Am I?"

"Yes. Or, I mean I think so. Someone else can make you decide to, but your the one who chooses who you are, no matter what anyone else says."

I smiled a little. **"Thanks Lacey. I love you."**

"Love you too. Glad I could help."

I wanted to think about all that. It felt important. But it was late, and just then, my head drooped down upon the warm ground and I drifted to sleep.

+++++++++++++

218

Andrea's quiet voice reached my ears early the next morning. "'You can get your chicks out, if you want.' -Dad."

My heart skipped a beat, already learning and understanding her riddles. *Hold us? Now?*

I braced myself, trying to remember Lacey's words from the night before. *Change yourself. No matter what anyone else says...* But it wasn't fitting in my sleepy mind. I couldn't just change myself, could I? Surely it wasn't that simple. This was who I'd always be. And soon my short time for dreaming ended. Her hands gently scooped me up. We sat on the cold, hard tile, Andrea letting us each down in front of her in the same gentle way. Lacey and Snowflake began to explore. I stared at my person.

She gently reached down and petted my

fluff. "Hi." She whispered softly. "'Can I hug?' -JoAnn Carol."

If I'd understood I'd probably have run away, but I didn't yet, so I still just stared. I wanted it all to stop for a minute so I could think. I didn't want to fall off her hands. I didn't want her to say that I didn't matter. And yet, I also wanted to see her heart.

She picked me up, slowly raising me until I was level with her face. The touch of a smile played at her lips.

"'You are a good little girl.' -Mom." I smiled a little then too, starting to relax.

But then there was something in her eyes, no behind her eyes. Like water. Different things in one place, around, backwards, mixed yet separate. And I looked away.

It was scary. It was different.

It was just like me.

Chapter 5
Different from the Rest: 225

I blinked my sleepy eyes open from my afternoon nap as the slender form appeared above us. "'Now is the time to be ready.' -Mark Willingson." She whispered in her riddles I had already grown more than used to in just over a week.

"Yes! I'm ready! I'm ready!" Snowflake chirped, then stopped abruptly. **"Wait, ready for what?"**

Andrea gave a small laugh as the chick spun around in circles. **"Outside, a little bit."**

For once, though not fearless, I was excited too, and entirely unaware that this day would stand forever a milestone in the flight from fear I was in.

Andrea carried me, cradled into both of her small hands, while her mom carried Snowflake and Lacey, each in one hand. Soon we were out the blue door and in the green, brown and blue and backyard. My eyes got wide as I gazed at all the grass, and a giant tree in the corner, a playhouse and swings set, and the sun on my slivery chick fuzz. It was like whole-new world being opened up to me. And beside the tree was a beginning of a structure. Little known to me it was our soon-to-be coop.

I closed my eyes contentedly embracing it all.

"Broooommmm…." something roared. And I panicked, happy feelings melting away all too quickly. I didn't know what to do. So I ran.

Then *everything* was wrong.

The world was in slow motion. I flapped my small wings. It was no use. I was falling and there wasn't anything I could do about it. I closed my eyes, and waited to collide with the hard ground.

But it never happened.

Instead, soft ground encompassed me. No, not ground, but gentle, loving hands embraced me before the ground had a chance. I was safe. *She had caught me.*

We were safe.

"Star!" Andrea exclaimed with a small but heavy breath. She gently hugged me and I welcomed it, gratefully. "Leaf-blower." She explained simply closing her eyes she breathed in deep. She sat down in the grass, keeping me on her lap. "'I love you, and I won't let anything hurt you.' -Lilian Kae."

I looked up at her. *She loved me.* And I realized, I loved her. To her, I *did* matter. I could trust her to catch me should I fall.

Andrea *was* certainly different. But *I* was different, too. *Everything* was different.

And I loved it.

Chapter 6
The Portal to Another World: 232

Andrea took us outside almost everyday after that, and today she sat down under the tree with a strange object in her hand. It was square, and it opened, to tons and tons more squares layered inside. I hopped over, no longer afraid of her much, at least when she was sitting still, and studied it further.

"Book." She stated simply, looking at my curiosity. She picked me up and set me on her lap so I could see the magic held within. A bright world stood before me, animals of all kinds leaped from the small box, and she turned over each square to flowers, trees, butterflies, and even chickens. Andrea found words in the book, and told a few to me. Quietly, she told me about the ocean.

I looked at the drawing, the huge body of water that was light blue closest to you and was a deep color on the father parts. White foam curled on the edges of the curling waves, and brown and white seagulls flew overhead.

Andrea read about storms, which knocked ships at sea. Waves hundreds of feet tall. Dark skies made the blue water into gray and black. Then the seagulls would leave. The happy white-tipped waves turned into deadly monsters, all because of a change; just a change on wind and weather. She explained this all to me in simple little slow and quiet phrases while I looked at the beautiful, soothing ocean in the book. How could what she was reading about, be that place? It looked so calm, peaceful, and something at the edge of the horizon, where the water stopped, made me want to go there, to run and reach that place where the world might be more true, so much bigger and brighter and we could see what the world really was. But, there would be storms before we could get there, I realized. No, we couldn't go there.

She set the book down slowly and leaned down beside me with a whisper: *"The ocean is scary."*

And she shuddered slightly. "'The waves could knock you down if you're not careful Andrea. Is the sand okay on your skin?' -Mom"

That was when I saw that she was scared, like I was. She was scared of it all. Even scared of herself. Like I was scared of me. She was trying to run away from it all too, longing for that distant horizon. *That* was what I'd seen in her eyes, even that very first day. It was like the storm, over her little ocean, beautiful, yet fearful; full of storms.

"I want to read to you more." Her hushed voice met my ears again as she closed the "book". I looked up into her amber eyes.

Sure enough, there I saw oceans.

Chapter 7
Enough to be Brave: 233

Something had gone wrong. I could see it right away in her eyes.

Andrea ran to our box, and normally she walked slow, and she was sobbing and blinking her eyes. **"What's the matter?"** I asked her, though I knew she couldn't understand. She hardly even looked at us before she squeezed herself into the corner beside us and sat shaking and crying. I thought perhaps I should be scared, she could hurt me, but my heart instead went out to her.

She wrapped her arms around herself, and began to rock back and forth. I cheeped at her and she looked at me, a wild and terrified look in her eyes, and she almost looked surprised that I was there, looking at her as she looked at me. The wildness slowly dissipated and she picked me up gently, stilling her shaking and flicking fingers to stroke my back, slowing her breath and quieting herself.

"'It's not my fault.' -Charlie." She finally whispered, her voice barely audible. But more water flowed from her eyes.

I nuzzled her, not sure what else to do. My heart pounded and I was scared for her… and myself, being in her hands. Her screaming and shaking threw me off. Surely I couldn't be scared of *her*. She was Andrea. But was this

Andrea? Something was wrapped around her, like it was trapping her from what I thought she was. It wasn't her strange movements, flicking her fingers and making strange sounds, it was something else that was trapping her, I just wasn't sure what. She whimpered, snapping me out of my thoughts. I tried to leap off her hands. She was scaring me. But she pulled me back, though gently, and started calming herself again. "' I don't want to be alone.' -Olivia Fern." She held me tight to her chest. There was disparity in her voice, and when I met her eyes, I saw the oceans again, fierce and crashing, a storm over the beauty. She was scared and confused, just like me. I'd only known her for a few weeks and already she was the most amazing person I'd ever met. Did she need help? *My* help? I forgot my fears. She was still Andrea. She was just trapped I guess, somehow. And somehow, I'd get her out. Not from the oceans, the oceans made her herself, but out of the storms, I'd at least help her through. I looked up at her ocean filled eyes, **"It's okay. Don't be scared. I'll...I'll help you, somehow."**

She looked down at me and almost smiled, though there was still a faraway look in her eyes. But then she frowned again and put me away. I sighed. My fears creeping back before I even took my next breath.

+++++++++++
237
Andrea remained, well, odd for the next

few days. She didn't say anything at all, and she constantly wore a scared look on her face. I tried in vain to figure out why, it had been a long shot to help anyways. And I gave up almost entirely.

And yet that was when the first sparks of the miracle began. She took us to the coop, now finished, every morning now, to let us have room and sun, the box becoming too small. And she was starting to smile and laugh a little, saying a word or two to us while she sat with us for awhile. And yet each day, she'd be gone all afternoon, leaving us to enjoy the outside world, and returned again silent and scared. She came to hold us as soon as she returned, and again, her walls began to break down, but sometimes they stayed, firm and unmovable. Each day, when she seemed to be better, I renewed my determination. I *would* help her. Then she was worse, and I wasn't sure I could keep on fighting an apparently impossible battle. All I wanted to do was fix her. Then we'd reach the end of the ocean and everything would be beautiful. But I always saw the oceans in her eyes and mine, and decided, day after day, though I didn't know how many ups and downs we would face, how many times my resolution would be crushed, I would always keep on.

+++++++++++

Andrea was holding us outside, the bright sun dulled by overcast cloud, the hints of winter peeping into the chilly breeze. I looked at Andrea as I sat on her shoulder, her bright hair whipping around in the wind. She still acted strangely, but she was Andrea, and I loved her no matter what may come. She sat there, stroking my almost filled in feathers and staring into space. She had hardly spoken at all in the last several days, so I was surprised when she began to talk to me.

"'In a way we are each trapped in a box," She said, with a faraway sounding voice, "and the person we are cannot escape ourselves.' -Ann Joseph."

I cocked my head. Like we were most of the time, when we were inside? That kind of box?

She sighed and looked down at me. "'It keeps them all from seeing. And it takes a special person to see all the way to the heart. It keeps me from seeing myself.' -Jamie Kia" She leaned her head into my fluff.

"It's okay, Andrea. Just…learn who you are, no matter what people think." Came my eager response. She was talking! She was telling me about herself! She was answering my questions. Telling me what was wrong.

She sighed again. "I can't talk right." She still whispered, and taking long pauses between each word. "My autism gets in the way, I guess. But 'The way you smile, when I say your name, will make me say it again and again. The way that you want to know, will make it so I learn somehow.' -Jack Elliot." I cocked my head. What… what did she mean?

She didn't say anything else for several minutes, but seemed to be thinking hard, her lips moving before sound passed them. "Samson is mean." She finally said. "My

old school was…better." She stopped again "'People stare and stare, the people, why are they everywhere?' -Kiandra Tye. I wish I…." she could hardly finish, and yet her words seemed to be pouring out now, as if she'd been planning and planning to say this, considering it everyday, and had to tell someone. As well as if these few simple words were like a whole other world to her. "I wish I could just be who I am. I wish Charlie would come home. I wish Mommy and Daddy could still afford me going to the private school. I wish I'd stop drowning in my own sea." Her tears fell faster on my back as she stopped talking. When she sat quiet again, staring at the cloudy sky, I nudged her with my fuzzy head. I didn't think about fixing her. I didn't think about the ocean. I thought that I just loved this girl and she needed to know no matter how fierce the storm she would not be alone.

"It's okay, I'll, we'll get through this… somehow. " I didn't know how, but it we had to, somehow.

"We can be brave, together, can't we? We can face our fears, and worries, and, and be okay, right?"

She looked at me slowly and smiled. "Thanks Star." She said, wiping away her tears. "'Be strong and courageous, for the Lord your God will be with you wherever you go.'" She picked me up and hugged me into her warm cheek, "I love you."

That was when I learned about love. And love is enough to make anyone brave.

Chapter 8
Coming out to Help: 240

My world brightened as Andrea slowly seemed to be getting better, as if she was finally hauled out of the pit she had been struggling in. I quickly realized, however, that it was her normal. Every few weeks or so she would go through this silence, confusion, and sometimes even throwing fits of anger. Sometimes it was very mild, and sometimes much more extreme. It had been almost a month now since I'd met her, and in that short amount of time, at least I thought, I'd seen the highest mountains and deepest valleys in Andrea. And yet the mountains always got steeper and the valleys deeper that I believed they could be.

In our box, we could hear most of what was happening around the house, as it was almost getting too cold for us to stay outside until our feathers filled in, Andrea was gone, as usual, in the afternoon, when one day I heard voices. "Mike, what, what's the matter?" I heard Andrea's mom saying with a strained voice.

It was a long pause and a sigh.
"Mike what is it?"
"Susan, don't...don't worry. We'll be fine..."
"But what happened?"
"They... they let me go, honey. I lost my job." His voice became all too quiet.

Mrs. Johnson gasped. "But...but, *Mike!* The house, we...we already can't— I mean we had to quit Andrea's therapy and...and take her from her old school...and, oh...what are we going to *do?*"

"Calm down, honey. I...I know it looks bad. But, we'll get through it. I'll find a new job. Life will move on. Just don't tell Andrea yet, alright? She...she doesn't need to handle adult concerns."

"Why, if they knew how hard of worker you are..." She muttered.

"Don't be mad at them. They had to let me go..." he paused, "I'm too distracted to be a good realtor."

"Mike, you know, Charlie...he's fine. It's...not your fault. And Andrea and I, we're fine. Don't worry about us."

"We had to take her therapy, her school," He paused again, "her brother."

"It's not your fault."

"*Then who's fault is it?*" He let out a heavy sigh.

"Mike..." Susan's voice was gentle and pleading to her husband's raising one.

"Please, don't. I should have at least listened to him..."

"That's not the point. Charlie, well... so he chose to leave home. He was 18 and that's okay. What's the big deal?"

"That he left because I was so hard headed I couldn't explain things to my own son." His voice turned bitter. "And I chased away the only person who actually could have understood Andrea." He sighed again. "This has nothing to do with work, does it?"

"It's okay, Mike. I'll see about working too, okay? And in the meantime..." Mrs. Johnson's voice turned as soft as it could, "call your son."

++++++++++++

Andrea came home, and found me in a mixed up mood. **"There's something wrong, Andrea. Your parents...they're upset. I don't know what to do."** Perhaps it was good she couldn't understand me so I didn't spoil her good mood. Andrea seemed happy and carefree. Out of her normal struggles, and light with childlike-serenity. She hugged me and sat me on her lap, bringing Snowflake and Lacey outside too, who ran around in circles on the ground. I looked up into her clear, bright eyes, the waves splashing with a gentle spray that spread easily, calming my own worried heart. The two of us snuggled quietly for several minutes, knowing the other had much on their minds, thought not feeling the need to speak it. Yet I saw that she was thinking, dreaming and wondering going through worlds each one at a time, behind her bright, clear and golden eyes. So much goes on behind one's eyes. And I saw it all in her silent ways.

That was when it hit me. *"I chased away the only person who understood Andrea."* Person. I didn't know what person that was, but what about chicken? I saw that there was some sort of block between the rest of the world and Andrea. But I'd dodged it unknowingly. How come I could see, when everyone else seemed so blind? I was some sort of link between the two worlds: Andrea, and everyone else. Maybe in this chaos I found myself in the middle of, I *could* help. I, Star, could make a change.

And I looked up to the beautiful face, her bright curls folding around her shoulders as she stared up at the huge green tree we were beneath. Her thin, red lips, in the slightest hint of a smile, her long, thin fingers curled gently around my body. And her eyes, the color of honey, gentle yet keen. Seeing everything yet so rarely sought by the rest of the world. And then I looked away.

What was I thinking? What good could I do?

I was just a chicken. I stiffened against the doubts one last time, holding still to hope. Maybe I was just a chicken, but I was *her* chicken.

Let   me   think…

I want to say it all.

Life with autism is a hard life. It is for anyone. But especially for a ten-year-old girl, like me, with other struggles in her life. I don't really want to talk about those yet.

It's hard for me to imagine what it would be like to live as a 'normal' person. But I'd guess it's hard for others to know what it's like to be like me. So, I'll try my best to explain.

It seems like a curse. All of it. It's like everything that was meant to be good, it turned upside down and results in awful pain. Literal, physical pain. Someone merely bumping into me or tapping my arm can feel like I'm being electrocuted from my own bones, bouncing back to a dull ache on my arms.

Or puppies, for example, are cute, adorable creatures that everyone loves.

When a dog barks, it pierces sharply through my ears. And their fur, it feels like a thousand needles, stabbing my skin. All animal fur. Luckily, my hair is long and wavy, and somehow different enough to my brain that I don't mind it on my back. Besides, getting it cut off is like pins falling onto my back, each managing to stab me.

Apparently, for some with ASD, communication is very difficult. While I am not as good as the average person at communications, I guess I manage much better than some. I've forced myself to learn how to talk like a normal person. Memorized many quotes that help me say what I mean, I read so many books, learning so many quotes. I memorize the "normal". You say hello, give one your name, and don't interrupt. So that's what I do.

Sometimes noises just sorta blurt out of my mouth, especially when I'm nervous. The kids at school laugh at me when I do this, but after a year, they all got used to it. I wave my hands and fingers, but nobody minded that either. I guess I am getting into those "other struggles" now. At my old school, most everyone forgot I was even diagnosed. It's not like that at my new school. I don't think it ever will be. My clicking tongue and flicking fingers had become normal at my old school. And I became so comfortable, that none of that happened too often anyways. There's only 100 kids at the entire school, which is super nice for a kid like me. It was so small there was not even a special-needs-section or anything. I was just with everybody. With my friends, that is, if you wanted to call them that. Because that's where the real problems start.

I know how to respond to a simple conversation. Like, *"How are you today?"* I say, *"Good."* When one says. *"I like your shirt."* I respond, *"Thanks."*

"How old are you?" "Ten." "What's the matter, Andrea?" There. That's where it falls apart.

Mom asks me this all the time. Almost everyday. But what do I say? I've never known what was wrong. I know there's a lot of things wrong. I'm overly aware and have acute senses to everything around me. But I can't seem to understand myself. Emotions! They flirt this way and that in ways I can't understand, pricking me like needles inside, or cooling me gently like a splashing wave, but then they become too strong and they knock me down, steal my breath and burn my eyes. And then everyone asks why I'm crying, or what I'm laughing at.

But…I don't know.

There's no textbook answer to those questions. I can't read what it is.

So maybe I'm not good at communication, after all. I just have memorized what "normal" people talk like. None of it comes from me, and who I am.

How then could I have friends? With no one knowing who I truly am, because I truly do not know.

I guess I'm just a blue in an apricot world.

Once, I told Mom that.

But she didn't understand.

No one understands.

Because I speak a different language than anyone on the planet.

Chapter 10
A World Away: 243

I walked through the 128,246 square foot building, unlike the 42,035 square foot school I used to go to. The beige walls, the black and gray floors, the yellowy lights, my purple shoes. I flicked my fingers and imagined that it was empty. It was just me and the black and gray floors and the beige walls. There wasn't the hundreds of footsteps thundering in my head, along with the hundreds of conversations echoing. There wasn't the occasional acciden-tal elbow that sent panic and pain spiraling through me. It was just silence.

But, of course, it wasn't. They all were there. Samson was there, too.

"Hey, Andrea!" The voice that pierced my ears was anything but kind and welcoming.

Must you yell?

I kept my gaze upon the floor, though com-pletely aware of his deep green one upon me.

"Oh, sorry. I forgot you can't hear me."

I can hear you. I just…never mind.

"Try to be normal won't you?" He harshly pushed my flicking fingers back to my sides.

I sucked in a breath at his sudden touch and yanked myself away.

"Come *on*. It's not my fault Mrs. Liles told me to help you to your class. Sure I volun-teered but still, she *asked* me. Anyways, just quit being a freak already."

He didn't think I understood, did he? I did, and I was going to cry. Not like he cared. Not like anyone cared.

"I mean honestly, though. What is your goal here, exactly? To make people sorry for you?"

What is your *goal, dude?*

I started flicking my fingers again, trying to flick away the blur of senses coming at me like bombs.

"Stop that." He pushed my arms down again, with bit tighter of a grip. I yelped and jumped back, hitting the wall. I pushed myself into it. I needed that wall.

"Anyway, like I said, I'm *supposed* to be helping you to your class. So come on."

Why would you show me there?

The question must have never reached his ears. For he wrapped his hand around my wrist and pulled my arm. I let my legs come out under me and fell to the floor. I turned and faced the wall. My wall.

"Come on, weirdo. You're making a scene. And everyone is going to think it is my fault."

It is your fault.

I closed my eyes. It was okay. Soon, I'd be back home. Home to Mom. And away from Samson. Back with Star. Yes, with my little Star.

After a few moments of Samson trying to sweet talk me into coming, and a few bad names thrown in between I lifted myself from the floor and strutted ahead of him, my head facing the floor and counting the tile floors.

467. Here we were, history.

"You little brat." He pushed me teasingly, or so he made it look. I bit back tears and ran to my seat. The back row, the back corner. The 45th seat. I let my hair fall over my face and wrapped my arms around myself.

Soon, I'll be home. I whispered to myself. *Soon, I'll be home.*

+++++++++++++

I pushed past Mom, through the house, through the blue back door, across the green grass, to the burgundy chicken coop, where the chickens spent the afternoon. I opened the door and sat on my stump Dad had placed there for me.

The three birds tried to cackle, but it was still mostly chirps. I didn't look at them. It hurt too much to...think. But I was acutely aware of their eyes on me, curiosity in them. *Curiosity.* I fumbled over the word. Was that an emotion? Or was it an action? Or was it what sent me into spirals when I tried to figure out myself?

I sighed. It was all much too complicated.

Suddenly, I felt something soft upon my hand, not a sharp, pain filled feeling, but soft, like it was meant to be, I suppose. It was Star, rubbing her feathers on me. Something exploded inside of me. It was a cool feeling, like a soft light. A gentle, cool splashing in my storm tossed and turning mind. Without thinking, my arms reached down and scooped up her fuzzy, small body. She pressed her little head against

45

my body and then looked into my eyes, and I returned the gaze. It seemed to me as though she was searching for the part of me that never escaped my own mind.

Did she see the fear in my eyes? Did she also see the hope, and the longing to play and love, and be who people wanted me to be? If I only knew what that was.

She nibbled a freckle on my arm. She didn't want me to be what other people wanted me to be.

She wanted me to be me.

Chapter 11
I'm The Problem to Solve: 243

"Hello, Andrea. How was school today?"
Mom's kind voice and innocent question made
Samson flashed across my eyes. Him
pushing me, yelling at me.

I'm not yelling at you. I remembered him
saying. But he was. To me, he was.

Yes, you are. Please stop! Either nobody
heard me, or they just never listened. Maybe
I had to try to get the words through my lips,
but sometimes it was just too hard.

I stared at the soup, focusing on the tart
yet calming smell of the cooked tomatoes.
Then I focused on the *taste* of my tomato
soup-dipped grilled cheese. *How was school?*
The school part was good. I learned about
long division, and the civil war, as well as
photosynthesis.

That was fun to say, when it curled
around my tongue right. When the sound of it
didn't explode back into my head. It was long
and yet gentle, and had a fascinating meaning.

"Photosynthesis." I said slowly, putting all
of my mind into the pronunciation.

Mom nodded slowly. "Is that what you
learned about in science today?"

I copied her gesture, my head bouncing
up and down slow and rhythmically.

"Anything...else?"

"I love Star." The words felt so right. They had to come out. A cool wave splashed my heart.

Mom's lips curled into a smile. " I'm glad."

I nodded again, then glanced around the table and at the 2 vacant seats, and one was normally filled.

"Daddy?"

She lost her smile. Why did she have to lose her beautiful smile that smoothed the lines of worry, took away the part of her I hated. I hated it because I knew I caused it. *Just smile again, Mommy. Smile.* "He is…finding work." Her words interrupted my silent pleas.

I frowned. *Again?*

Her fingertips gently touched my cheek, but I leaped back, the feeling shocking me. She withdrew it. "Don't worry about it, sweetheart."

It was such a simple command, but so impossible to obey. Not worry. I never was trying to eavesdrop, but even from my room, when I was trying to sleep, their hushed voices came to me clearly. Dad needed a job. And it was my fault he did. I made him sad and worried. Why couldn't I make people *happy* for once? I was the problem. I made all the storms.

That was why I had to go to school with Samson now. Because my old school cost too much money. My time with Mrs. Carol was too much money. But if it weren't for her, I wouldn't even be able to understand there was a problem. She helped me talk, and understand. She helped me know what to do

when the pain was exploding through my head.
Mom stayed home most of the time, cleaning
my messes, and reading books, endless books,
on what to do about me. They were still
trying to figure me out, to stop my problems,
and theirs too. And then she had to pick me
up from school, since the school buses were
too loud. So painfully, deafeningly loud. I
shuddered at the thought of them.

Mom reached for my arm gently. "Are
you okay?" I snapped back to the present and
leaped back, an angry noise escaping from my
throat though I didn't mean for it to. I wrapped
my arms around myself and stared at my food
again, trying to find a feeling different from
all this. Less painful. I wasn't okay, I was
different. I made everybody else worried, or
angry, or sad, or something. All the feelings
mingled together into a big, painful heap I'd
never understand.

All I understood was all of it was my fault.

+++++++++++

"Andrea, don't forget to feed your
chickens." Mom said awhile later.

Cool waters washed over my thoughts.
Yes. I get to go see the chickens.

I stood up from the homework I'd just
finished and headed towards the door, slipping
into my new, black rubber boots. Mom said
they were my 'chicken shoes'. But they looked
nothing like chickens. Still, I wore them when
I went into the coop. I could feel Mom's smile

49

burning into my back, but the thought of returning it never came to my mind. I merely walked outside without a word, focusing my attention on the sensations I could name around me. Like the colors. Those had names. Places where I could put them. Blue door, green grass, burgundy coop. The familiar colors soothed my flicking fingers, always the same. Though the rough feel of the chicken feed agitated them again.

Your food feels gross. I thought to the chickens, *But I know you need your food, so I'll always give it to you. Don't worry. I'll always take care of you.*

I stuck my tongue out and wrinkled my nose as I cleaned the water dish, but soon the disgusting job was done, and it was time to snuggle. "Hey guys." My voice barely brushed past my lips, the silence seeming too precious to shatter, the peace in my head did not need to be ruined. Each of their eyes turned upon me. Snowflakes, a silvery blue, Lacey's a deep gray, and Star's a dark shade of brown. My gaze halted onto hers. Something splashed in them. Something like the eyes I saw in the mirror. The waters of fear and longing for…something. But other times tickled and played, that washed away the storms. And again the waves that crash over one's head with no warning. Star's, however, wasn't an infinite water she was drowning in. Her's was a bluster of a storm. A storm that could be quickly blown away. Yet how can such massive, roaring hurricanes as I was facing be destroyed? Such oceans of water? Wait, put down anchor and wait. But when would they stop? The waters poured over me again now. The delicate balance of when calm becomes storm, splash becomes waves, fun becomes terror. Would the waters ever be calmed? I shuddered and covered my eyes sinking to the ground. It was inescapable and I knew it. My eyes shot open as gentle feathers nudged my arms, and weight settled itself on my lap. Star and Snowflake sat beside me, Lacey on me, a twinkling splash in each of their bright eyes. A splash I'd later name as sympathy. And it took just some of the waters away.

After only a month, actually, 27 days, they had come to trust me so easily. They pecked a chirped as happy as anything could be. I tried to imagine what it must have felt like, that particular droplet of hope that seemed so rare now. Mom had labeled it 'happiness' for me. Sometimes it was nice to have the names, just for the sake of communicating. But for them it must have been more than a droplet. An ongoing rolling, gentle waves, turning the sand, sifting their thoughts, keeping them living and thriving everyday, washing away their fears.

"Why can't people be like chickens?" These words brushed past my lips, somehow sneaking out from my trapped mind. I let my hand brush over the reddish brown feathers on Lacey's back and she let out a small, happy chicken noise. Although no more words could make it out through my lips, I felt the feelings in my fingertips as they brushed the chicken's back.

"Sometimes, people don't like you because you're different. Like a chicken isn't a dog, so people don't like them as much. But dogs have poky hair. Chickens have soft feathers. They're different, but they both matter.

Maybe to some people, like Samson, I have poky hair." A sort of laugh escaped my throat at my own connection. *"Not actually poky, of course, but, I don't know somehow, like dogs are poky, so they scare me, but chickens are different, so they don't...then I'm different, and I'm poky to Samson. Maybe."* I stopped and bit my lip, then shook my head vigorously, so that all the thoughts and feelings blended together. They weren't colors. They were thoughts and feelings. They had no places. I wanted them to go back away. *"All I ever do is make problems, not solve them. I am Andrea. I don't solve problems. I don't understand things and figure them out. I just make the problems."* I sighed and pushed Lacey off my lap; she shouldn't love me. Tears splattered onto my lap as I stood. *"And neither these chickens or me will ever do anything to solve those problems."* And I went inside, to let myself be trapped alone. I couldn't let anyone else be trapped too.

Star

Chapter 12
A Star in the Night Sky: 246

"I don't know what to do, Lacey." I sighed one bright afternoon, watching Andrea go inside, leaving us to get some room and sun. "Do about what?"

"Andrea. She needs me."

"You need yourself. To calm down, that is."

I cocked my head. "What?"

"Never mind." Lacey shrugged as Snowflake danced over to us.

"Happy Birthday to WE! Happy Birthday to WE!!"

"What are you talking about, Snowflake?" I asked her.

"We're a month old today, according to Andrea! And we're not going back to the smelly, little crowded box any more, because....HAPPY BIRTHDAY TO WE! HAPPY BIRTHDAY TO WE!!!"

My heart sank a little, the coop wasn't too bad, but the news of moving didn't help my mood. Snowflake danced back across the coop, still singing. I tried to laugh, and then shook my head clearing my thoughts again. Turning back to Lacey I continued, "I'm just not good enough, Lacey. I-I don't even know what to do. How to help...What ever it is she needs help with."

"Star," Snowflake, suddenly back, nudged me before Lacey could speak, **"You're like the super-awesomest chick I've ever met, and I don't know why to cawack so much about the simplest things!"**

"Cawack?" I questioned her, confused.

"Yeah, like you're doing right now. Being all serious because you're so worried about letting people down you won't just be you. The happy, normal real you, without all the cawackiness."

And she sent me to silence by the spark in her eyes, and the part of my little sister I had never seen before; the part that saw right through me.

"Besides," She continued, **"I didn't tell you the best part about our birthday."** She made an odd face, attempting to conceal her excitement.

"What is it?"

"Tonight, Andrea and her whole family is going to come outside and have a picnic for dinner! And we get to be frange!" She began dancing again.

"It's called free-range." Lacey giggled.

"FRANGE!" She yelled, enjoying the word.

"Sure, why not?"

I looked at the happy dancing, fuzzy bird. The one I'd loved since I'd met her, and had been my sister ever since too. And I realized she had helped me, without being worried. But an honest innocence that gave her vision through any mask. And somehow shown that my fear was blocking me from doing the every thing I was attempting. It was keeping me from love. I was trying too hard to do it myself and make it all be right to see what Andrea actually needed and just be there for her.

So I shook off my "cawackiness" and looked forward to the evening. I let go of fear and grasped onto love.

+++++++++++

I watched the coop door open, with my sisters by my side. What was it that made us all prickle at the simplicity? The air, that seemed contagious with a splash of bright: it was happiness, wasn't it? Snowflake bolted out the moment there was a gap big enough, hopped up and down in front of Andrea and then kept running, trying out her newly-found cackle, still a high pitched with a shrill chirp in the middle. I listened to the laughter bubble from the girl's heart, and smiled. I loved this place so much. I trotted over to my person, and tried my cackle, but it came out more like a chirp as well. Andrea flicked her fingers a few times, like she oftentimes did, and sat down on the fresh grass. I hopped onto her lap, and she stroked my feathers, apparently deep in thought, yet her attitude was not closed off, not in another world and scared to open up, but a sort of open thoughtfulness, looking at the world and letting it look at her.

"Andrea, come eat your dinner, sweetie." Andrea's mom called from across the yard, and

I hopped off to explore on my own.

Soon, as I wandered the world turned into a bright fiery red as I'd never seen it before. A golden light was dancing between the trees, and sparkling on Andrea's own golden waves of hair. The sun lowered slowly, the time Andrea usually brought us inside. Indeed, even the sparrows flew to their homes, and I settled down onto the cool grass, closing my eyes, and going to sleep…

I opened my eyes. But I could see nothing but darkness. Nothing was before me. Nothing behind me. Where was I?! Surely the grass was under my feet, for I felt it, but all was black. There was a small glowing circle far above my head, but it only confused me farther. **"Snowflake!"** I screamed in desperation, **"Lacey!"** I jumped and spun around to no avail. Worst of all it let the fears I'd always been fighting slip back in all too easily. It was a despairing world, lost and hopeless. I had nothing against the swirling unstoppable darkness. *You're just a chicken*. The silence whispered. *You are alone.* It haunted me. Was it the darkness? Or was it myself? *You can't do it. You'll mess it all up. No one cares about you.* And then I saw something walking towards me, a faint outline, the deepest of darkness, approaching me. Then another voice, that was not my own reached me:

"Hey, Star, it's okay." That was when I saw the waves of golden hair, and then, yes, it was. My Andrea. It was the twinkling of her bright, amber eye. "'When it's dark, I'll help you see.'" She sang softly to me. Her slim hands encompassed my frazzled self, and carried me over to a light, on the other side of the yard, where her parents were still chatting. Snowflake and Lacey sat together, too. The darkness was pushed away.

My racing heart slowed. We were all fine, it was just me, cawacking again. Andrea kept us safe. And in the dark I saw the thing I'd been running away from, the thing I'd been so scared of facing, had been myself, and the things I couldn't do. And the one who saved me from myself—why, I was sitting in her arms! She always fed us just when we needed our food. I leaned into Andrea's warm body, and felt her heart racing, too. I'd scared her, freaking out like that. And now her brown eyes showed tears. And so did mine.

We sat. And we cried together, the pains and fears finally hitting us, through our walls and leaving through a river of tears. I don't think either of us knew why, and we still don't. Mr. and Mrs. Johnson sat a ways away, still talking after their dinner, by the light. My friend and I were on the fringes of the darkness yet. I was not scared though. After all, I saw it was never the darkness I was scared of, or the loud noises, or falling. I was scared of myself, to be who I am. Too scared to let anyone down, so I wouldn't get up, or help anyone up, and we'd never fall. I leaned against Andrea, and we let ourselves, and let our wills, go. We turned towards the thing we ran from. Not the amazing, uplifting moment that was yet to come, but the moment that we both, somehow in the same moment, let the hard, outer layer of our shells crumble away, the hard stuff we'd been trying to be, back to who we were. Deep, in ourselves, and our cawackiness, disappeared. No one spoke, but our minds were the same. *"I have been running from love and trust, from hope and happiness. Things I didn't think could be mine because I am just a chicken… I am just a girl with autism. But that's okay. Because…*I stopped, my very thoughts halted, before I knew how to even think the rest. Then it hit me. *Because there is something greater than us, that makes us matter. And even if Andrea was not there to give us the food, there must be something bigger than that, something that brought us together. And I do matter, because* you *matter.* And that moment, a deep wash flooded me. A warm, strong and rushing water poured over me and cleansed me of my fears. Because, I'd understand more fully later, that there *was* Someone who cared for us all, big and small, autistic, and, well, chickens. And that because of Him, I *could* be enough. Because He cared about Andrea, she cared about me, and I cared about her, so I could care for myself. And a peace like I'd never felt before rested on me. And I rested on Andrea in silence.

+++++++++++

It was only a few moments after those life changing thoughts that life changing words and sights followed them. With new eyes I looked at my friend, and hers met mine. They were not swimming. Not drowning in oceans. But a cool splatter, like rain on a hot day, pure and peaceful. Her eyes were true. And so were mine.

Then the words crossed her lips, methodically like the silent wind, the sound of the darkness, not shattering the silence, but merely laying a finger upon it.

"Star," the words came, "look." I obeyed, turning my head upward where she pointed to a deep and endless darkness, in which nothing could be seen. It was lost, empty and hopeless. I turned my head away quickly. But she gently lifted my chin until I again faced the scary sky.

I faced the darkness that seemed to grow closer each second. Deeper and darker and... wait, what was that? It was a bright...light! Halted in the very middle of the darkness, not being sucked in, not being thrown out, just suspended there; bright and twinkling with nothing to be anxious of. My breath caught: there were more! As the minutes passed, my eyes sought more and more, and they were found. Each shedding its own bit of light, making the sky, this dark and different version of the sky, not so inky and dreadful, but beautiful. I cast my awestruck face to gaze at Andrea, her gaze also turned to the sky. Her amber jewels fixed on the bright, twinkling ones, but her voice reached me once again; and each time her voice reached me, I laughed inside, her voice so song like and yet never used. Used only when she really needed to, and now was most certainly one of those times. It was not just words, it was a song:

"The world is dark," she rocked back and forth to an imaginary tune,

"Sometimes it is really dark." Her voice rose and fell methodically, .

"And we can't seem to chase that darkness away…"

"And in our brokenness, He sees beauty." She closed her eyes and hummed a little.

"But He loves us He makes us enough." Her bright eyes closed.

"And in this darkest night, He uses our brokenness to make sta…rs." Pause.

"He made us who we are, He made us broken, to be whole as stars."

Her eyes were still fixed on the night sky.

"And when He is in our hearts, we shine like lights."

"Lights that make us new, and that everyone can see in the darkness of life."

A long pause met my ears as her song ended and we stared upwards, when again her voice touched the silence, "I think God put a light in you, that I found in the darkness of myself." She stopped just for a moment, finding the words,

"A star in the night."

She looked at me, and her lips curled into a little smile. "Those," She pointed up, "are stars." I smiled back, and I knew who I was.

Chapter 13
Into Her World: 249

Fear had faded into a little-noticed mist. Love had become air, water, wind and life. And I loved; I was loved and I loved. Life was beautiful, and I thought nothing could ever change that beauty. And perhaps in the end, I was right; it just was just a little bit more complicated than that.

But then came the day when Andrea came to me with the oceans back in her eyes. Two separate oceans, intermingled with one another. On the outside the glassy layer of tears, but deep behind that was the ocean I'd come to know as a world of fears and worries more complicated than any words could ever explain. But I could almost feel it. It was like a finger on a wound that I'd forgotten was still sore. Now, I watched the sullen and tearful Andrea dealing with it still, the wound still fresh and stinging, seeming to be torn open again and again. She had followed an ear-piercing scream from the house, a screech, it seemed, that could not be controlled. Now, however, all was silent as she sat under a tree, while Snowflake, Lacey and I roamed the grass. I watched her tears rolled freely, as I came and sat beside her. Then the scream cut through the air again, and to my shock, it came from Andrea! Who knew she could make such a horrible sound! But, why? Then she began banging her head on her hands and yelping out noises. I needed to hear or say no words. Something was wrong. I gently hopped onto her legs, hoping to comfort her. Just as I landed, the screech hit my ears again, and she pushed me off. The pain of my own Andrea's rejection whirled inside of me; *why did she do that?* But surely that wasn't truly Andrea who just pushed me away, Andrea was not like that. It was the crashing of the waters that her eyes swam in; a storm, on a beautiful plain like in her books: dark, scary, and whirling, on top of the tranquility of the leaves, the green grass, the blossoming wildflowers, the distant rocky peaks, and beyond that, the oceans, calm and still, taking the rain and the winds back to their crashing waters.

Then her eyes met mine, the waters lulled, and her lip began to quiver. She scooped me up ever so softly and held me close, her wet tears soaking into my feathers. I didn't move, but buried myself into the precious embrace.

+++++++++++

Andrea was strapping a papery object on my backside that smelled sweet and mellow and had straps apparently to make it stay on me, though it was big in some places, and tight in other places, made for something other than a chicken, it seemed. An excited spark lit her eyes as she stopped messing with it and nodded at me, having fitted it as best she could. I shook my uncomfortable feathers and cackle-chirped at my owner.

"Why is this on me? Why?"

She frowned at my antics and kneeled back down, gently stroking my feathers and humming. I suppose it wasn't that uncomfortable, I sighed to myself.

The little girl proceeded to pick me up and carry me…into the house! I got to go back in the house? Why, I'd just moved outside a few weeks ago!

"Have fun Star!" Snowflake called.

I smiled, though a familiar fear flickered in my chest, today, however, it was mingled with excitement, for something told me this wasn't going to be a normal day, and that maybe my hopes were coming true, maybe we were making it to the horizon after all.

We walked through the door, and into Andrea's bedroom, a bright, big room with blue walls, a table with paints on it sat in the corner, and a big bed on the other side and other small things through out the room. Setting me down, she picked up some blocks and I saw the extravagant city on the floor. There were little roads, tall buildings rose up in the middle and smaller houses scattered the edges, and each block was perfectly centered on top of another. I hardly took all this in before we began playing, I pecking a block, Andrea putting it on a building. Then I'd wander through the city, finding small trees, a blue house, or following the tiny winding road. All while Andrea would click her tongue, pet me, and build more, occasionally humming a tune. I'd explore the bed, with flowers on the blankets, not flowers you could eat of course, but still fun. I also found her stuffed toys, lined up beneath her blanket, like a real person would be. She had small LEGOs, that she refused to let me even taste, of course. I hopped on her desk. And I gazed around, I saw another chicken! Wait, wait, no. It was me. A reflection of me. I soon walked back to Andrea, who smiled and picked me up, hugged me, and sat on her bed and sat me down beside her, so I wandered again, with her eyes on me. A giggle escaped her when I tried to eat another flower. They were all inedible, I soon realized. Then I looked back. Her smile warm and true, honest and full. This, this was love. It was friendship, and, even with the paper contraption, it was one of the best moments I'd ever felt.

+++++++++++

253

Andrea took me inside the house often, after that day. She took Snowflake and Lacey in too, but neither of them appreciated the paper too much. And Andrea explained we *had* to wear it, so we didn't "mess up" the house. She even wiped our feet all clean, and gently spritzed us with water and rubbed us until we shone.

"I don't get it, Star." Lacey chuckled one day, **"You were all scared of everything on the planet, and now you let Andrea do just about anything to you, all with a smile on**

your face!"

I giggled back, "I guess it's called trust, Lace'. Its being a star. Besides, you know she wouldn't hurt you."

"Yeah, I know. She's the gentlest, sweetest girl I've ever seen. But, well, I need my feathers free! And dirt on my toes, and my feathers dry."

I smiled at her contentedly. "It doesn't bother me a bit."

"What's happened to you, sis? I like it, whatever it is." She rubbed her beak against me lovingly.

"Like you said, I had to learn to be myself. From now on, I really am me."

"I thought we got rid of that, now that we have names?" Snowflake leaped on top of us from the perch above our heads. We both cackled as a flurry of feathers flew. "Sorry, I didn't look." Snowflake said meekly.

Lacey and I just giggled.

"So why are you going back to 'me'? I thought you were Star now."

"Oh, I am Star. I am just myself now, I guess. The playful, happy, loving chick I was meant to be. Not, well, whatever I was."

"Cawacky?"

"Yeah, cawacky."

"One thing though, Star." Lacey pointed out, "I don't think we're exactly chicks anymore. We're pullets. Nearly two months old!"

I laughed pure heartedly. "Well chick

or not, I want to play! C'mon Snowflake!" I leapt at her feet and she leaped over my head, being small but agile, and was behind me now. I raised my feathers and screeched my biggest, non-chirpiest cackle I could before we dashed around the coop in circles.

"I want in!" Lacey announced, joining the random chase.

In fact we were playing so hard that when I halted Snowflake and Lacey both ran into me and crashed to the ground. Composing ourselves, I turned towards the noise I heard. Sure enough, it was the soft footstep of Andrea. She giggled lightly. "Play?" She looked at me, and held up the diaper. I scrambled back to my feet and ran over to the door, waiting for her to open it.

Lacey and shook her head while Andrea prepared me, with all her methods of cleaning and prepping and getting me ready. **"Have fun, sis."** My sister sighed happily, **"though I wouldn't."**

I smiled, before I was out of sight and inside.

There was a new building, in Andrea's city today. Andrea worked very hard at it. It looked like, well, in fact, it looked like me! But as we played silently, as Andrea preferred, I happened to hear a conversation in the other room.

"Mike, you know why." Andrea's Mom's voice came, sounding upset.

"Yes, I suppose I do. But what can we do to change it, that's what I don't know."

"We could tell the teacher she can't do the show and tell. It would be that simple."

"Her new school is not her old one, Susan." Mr. Johnson's voice returned.

"I know, but surely they'd understand, right?" She persisted

"No. They might listen but *no one* actually *understands* autism. Besides…" He tapered off.

"What?"

"Its all we can do to stop the world from seeing her for…what she *has*, not what she *is*."

"It's not a disease, Mike."

"But it's not *her* either. Some people have brown hair, some people blonde. Some people are on the spectrum, some people aren't!" He let out a heavy sigh. "It's part of her, but it's not who she is."

"What does this have to do with the show and tell?"

"That if we say "She can't do it. She's autistic." Every kid in her class will see this one girl didn't do it. And we know Andrea *notices* those kind of things. She wants to be with them, Susan. She just wants them to understand."

There was a long pause. "Did…did she—tell you that?" Andrea's Mom, Susan, responded quietly.

"She'll write sometimes, honey. Just on her own time."

Another long pause. I could almost see Mrs. Johnson with her palm over her face, thinking. Then her voice came again. "So what do you think we should do?"

"Help her. Let her practice. She *can* do this show and tell."

"But with what, Mike? She screeched for a day just hearing about it. What can she go in front of everyone and talk about?"

It made sense to me then. Why she'd been so upset the other day.

"Well let's just ask her," And I heard foot steps and leaped away from the door to my friend's lap.

"Hey Andrea—" His gaze halted on me. "Why is the chicken in the house?"

"What?!" Mom ran to the door as well, where I looked out from Andrea's lap

innocently. "It's gonna poop all over the house!"

"No, she won't." Andrea held me up, showing the diaper calmly, clearly not thinking there was any reason I *shouldn't* be in the house. I surely didn't think there was either.

Mr. Johnson shook his head. "Is that a *diaper*?"

Andrea nodded, her eyes twinkling.

He turned to his wife. "Where did she find a newborn's diaper?"

"I — I had some in the closet."

"For *10 years*?"

"Yeah." She said, laughing.

He shook his head again, "Well, they're in good use. They just helped solve our problem."

"What problem?" Mrs. Johnson asked.

"People use pets for show and tell all the time. Andrea can take Star."

Susan laughed sounding like a weight was lifted from her shoulder. "Yes! Absolutely!" Before shaking her head and looking at me. "But the poor thing will need something that looks less ridiculous than that old diaper to wear if she's leaving our house."

Chapter 14
Butterflies: 256

The wind tousled with my feathers, Andrea's long hair falling into my face every few minutes. I looked up at her bright eyes, which were fixed upon the book she was reading in the bright, cool afternoon. I looked from her eyes to the paper they looked at, and saw a bright picture of a butterfly, along with a picture of a strange little green thing. "Metamorphosis." Andrea read aloud, "A larvae," she pointed to the wriggling worm photo, "turns to a pupae, turns to a chrysalis," her finger glided to the green thing, "and emerges as an adult." Her finger lay on the orange butterfly that seemed to fly off the page. I thought about it for a moment. I wondered why it seemed so familiar, the whole thing. That a puny little larvae, would *change*. That word struck me, and I looked up into the happy face, her cheeks rosy, her red lips turned up, and her golden hair cascading over her shoulders; picturesque in the sunny green yard. Not the girl clinging to her dad, her hair a tangle, and her face pale and overwhelmed. And then I considered myself. My black and white feathers thick upon my small body, a bright comb adorning my head now, and my chick stripes and fuzz long gone. But there's more than that that had changed. She spoke more a little more each day, my fear faded a little more, too. And I saw that it was fear she was facing too, even if it looked different. There was never a day when everything changed. But now, sitting on Andrea's lap, looking at a butterfly, I saw everything had. And now, she was taking me to school tomorrow. To *help* her. In all my cawackiness, my own little struggles, I had helped her. Her lips moved, reading the words on the paper, when before her tongue lay still. When did she start? Word by word, day by day, she'd changed. And somehow, so had I. In my eyes, we were butterflies.

Chapter 15
Why Did the Chicken Go to School?
258

My heart thumped nervously as I faced
the unknown. I had said bye to Snowflake
and Lacey, although Andrea assured me it was
only a few hours before we'd be back. And,
now sporting my fancy new harness Andrea's
mom had bought for me, and we each had
one. Snowflakes a light lavender, with little
white flowers; Lacey's a beautiful turquoise
blue, with yellow stripes; and mine a deep
scarlet red, with white polka dots. And, to be
honest, it was *much* more comfortable than
the baby diaper I had been wearing inside. In
fact, neither Snowflake nor Lacey minded it
much. Still, I'd been chosen for *this* adventure.
Andrea held me close and we loaded in the car.
My mind raced back to those months ago when
I'd been a teensy chick in a box, being taken to
a new home in that same car. I laughed quietly
at my own silliness back then, seeming ages
ago, though it seemed to remain like a faded
echo never fully erased. Now, however, was
something completely different: I was going to
school. Andrea was going to take me in front
of the whole class, and show me to the other
students. There was so much to think about for
that upcoming moment.

I focused on Andrea's gentle hand on my

feathers, rubbing gently. I could tell she was nervous, but also excited that I was coming. When the short ride was over, she let me walk beside her, holding onto the leash tightly.

I saw people swarm in and out of the large building ahead. None of them noticed me; at least not yet. Andrea tensed up as she set me on the concrete, she turned to her mom, and she smiled a small, forced smile.

Mrs. Johnson's eyes sparkled as she petted her daughter's hair, returning the smile, "You'll do great, sweetheart." She swallowed hard, "you'll do great."

Andrea's gaze quickly left her mom's and darted to the ground. "Thank you. 'I just wish I could know how to be all you are.' -Nick Lloyd. Bye."

And my friend turned and walked away, but I looked back just in time to see her mom's hand fly to her mouth and her eyes widen; a tear dripped from her shocked face. I hurried back to Andrea after a glance, but I knew that was the first time Andrea had said goodbye to her mom that way. I also knew it wouldn't be the last.

++++++++++

We only walked a few paces before Andrea scooped me back up again. She whispered that she didn't want anyone to step on me, but we both knew that she needed me in her arms just then. I happily snuggled my head into her chest and felt her relax slightly. Then I focused on my surroundings. The black floors. The beige walls. The lights above my head were too bright, with a yellowy tint. I liked the sunlight better.

And then there were the people.

There must have been hundreds. Thousands perhaps. They echoed through the whole building. Back and forth, towards us, away from us. Boys and girls, tall and short, with all different colored eyes. We walked next to the wall, and Andrea kept one hand on it, sinking away from anyone who passed. Once someone bumped us: Andrea froze and pressed herself against the wall. I nudged her gently, but she refused to move. Finally, I hopped out of her arms and began walking till the leash was tot. Her eyes met mine and the water subsided. She stepped forward, and began to walk again.

It was all like a dream. No information came from hearing. That sense was temporarily blocked from my mind. Too many strange sounds rendered it useless. I just used my eyes. I watched as Andrea picked me up again, I watched the people walk, talk and stare. I watched the world go by in a chaotic blur. Then I watched Andrea's eyes. They stayed glued to the floor. The black tiles, and the gray ones. Then I watched her mouth, it moved ever so slightly. And I tried again to use my ears, focusing gone her quiet whisper:

"562…563…564… 565…"

She was *counting* them. I kept watching

her, trying to ignore the overwhelming environment until we made it to 742. There, we stopped just in front of a door, which she opened and walked through, found a desk and sat down.

No one said a thing to us, they just stared, hardly trying to hide it, and my friend and I just snuggled, ignoring the many pairs of eyes, until the class started.

Soon, however, a lady starting talking, glancing at me sideways occasionally. Her words swished past my mind, and I kept my eyes on Andrea's face. Then the woman said Andrea's name.

"Andrea Johnson, it is your turn to have your show and tell! Please come tell us what you've brought."

Andrea swallowed, took a deep breath and looked down at me, "'Take the leap.' -Mariah Kay."

Then she stood before the crowd. It was only maybe about 40 or so kids. "43." Andrea mouthed, giving the exact number. But that made 86 eyes on us. Plus the teacher's, so 88— of course I can't do math. Andrea told me. She looked at me, gave a small smile, and looked back up:

"This is Star. She's my chicken. I have three chickens: Star, Lacey and Snowflake. They are each very different. And Star is the snuggliest. Snowflake's excitable. And I think Lacey is the smartest." She looked down at me, she winked at me, making sure she didn't offend me. Then she took a deep breath, and, unlike she had practiced at home, poured a bit of her heart out.

"'My song is not the song of the world. Mine is the voice of another. But perhaps we all come from our own little places, and all have our own little dreams. So please, not again, please don't run away from me.' -Lillian Jackson." She bit her lip, and slowed her before rapid and rambling speech: "don't be scared of me because I'm different. And don't be scared of Star." Then she practically ran back to her seat.

"Star." She murmured in my feathers when the teacher started to talk again, "I am never *ever* doing that again." And with that she buried her face into my feathers and didn't look back up.

When the class was over, Andrea leaned against a wall, her face halfway turned to it, a misty ocean rain in her eyes after her speech, but her fingers lay still at her side. I looked the out as kids meandered out of the room, chatting with one another. One girl caught my attention. She had bright hair and swished this way and that when she walked, and her light blue eyes, surrounded by a thousand freckles. She wore a black and white stripey shirt; I noticed, because it was the same color as me. And also because she was walking towards us.

"Hi!" She said in a high, bright voice, "I'm Penny. I *love* your chicken. My aunt and uncle have chickens, but Mom says we can't in our neighborhood. I can't imagine why. Their darling and I can't imagine they'd bother a body. Can I pet her?"

Andrea looked down at me, a world beyond in them, and then she turned her terrified yet overjoyed, sparkly eyes towards Penny. "Yes."

Penny gingerly reached out her hand and rubbed my feathers gently. "She's *so* soft." Then she shook her head. "Boy, I talk too much. What's your name?"

"Andrea." My girl whispered, I nudged her arm to boost her confidence.

Penny's voice turned gentle. "Hey, I don't want to bother you. Do you want me to leave you alone?"

"No." Andrea's voice was quick and louder. "Stay, please."

"Okay, you want to walk to my next class with me?"

"Yes."

"C'mon." She made contact with Andrea's hand, who yelped slightly and pulled it back. "Oh, I'm sorry. Did I hurt you?"

Andrea stayed silent for a minute, "Yeah, but 'all they do is tear me apart, but still they will not shatter my heart.' -Kia Jones."

Penny bit her lip, obviously set back by the small glimpse into how different this girl she was talking to was. But she quickly overcame it, quicker than anyone else ever had. "Um, so, how old are you?"

"10." Andrea was quiet again, and

reached her hand down and scratched my feathers. "You?"

"I'm 11, but I was ten a week ago. It was my birthday on Monday."

"Happy birthday."

"Thanks! It was super fun. My party is on Saturday." She paused and bit her lip again, "I want you and Star to come. I mean I just met you like 5 minutes ago, but, yeah." She laughed. "I'm really annoying, huh?"

"No. I like it when you talk. Your voice is pretty."

Her face turned pink, "Really? No one ever tells me that. I had a speech imp-ed-u-ment, or something, when I was younger, and I guess I still do. So it's like I have an accent, but I don't. I just don't talk right." She laughed again, "but I'm glad you like it."

I looked up and saw that spark in Andrea's eyes: happiness, or excitement. But she kept quiet. So Penny started talking again. "When is *your* birthday?"

"301."

"301? What does that mean?"

Andrea started clicking her tongue and held me a little tighter. "My birthday." She finally blurted, uncomfortable at the reminder that she was so hard to understand by everyone.

"You're birthday is...256." Andrea added.

"What?"

Andrea shook her head, "My class is here."

"Alright. I'll ask my mom if you can come to the party. Bye, Andrea, bye Star." I cackled my farewell, and Andrea waved before flicking her fingers, her heart still banging in her chest after talking, having a *conversation* with someone. I wasn't *always* with Andrea, of course, but I knew that was beyond her comfort, and I admired her bravery. This certainly was not a day I'd soon forget, I knew.

I was busy musing on this when a screech and jerk surprised me. A screech from *my* person. I looked and saw a boy, with jet black hair, a few inches taller than Andrea, and pulling her arm.

"Come on, I've been looking for you, to help you to class. Why'd you run off?"

She squeezed me and squirmed from his grip. "I-I don't need help. I-I know w-where I am going." The words were stiff and robotic as she marched into the classroom, and I saw it took every last ounce of bravery she had.

"Yeah, well, you're obviously not capable of going to your class and obeying the school rules like a normal person. We don't mess with our fingers like that, or, or bring *chickens* to school."

"For show and tell." Her all too clear words returned, sounding small.

"Yeah, I know. I saw your silly show. I was in the room, you know."

"Yes, I do."

"And so you proved to us all that this is a ridiculous act. You really don't belong here, you know. Sorry, we're not scared of you. We just don't like you. You'll never be like us.",

That's when I felt it. The cold, wet tear that no one ever saw, but fell onto my back. My Andrea was crying because of this...this... cawacky kid who thought he was "helping", or whatever. He didn't see who Andrea was, he wanted to be what he was not because he was scared of what he was. So he had his own wall, and he was breaking her down along with a part of himself. Breaking down the hope she'd built up. Breaking her very self, and if he didn't stop, all the beautiful trees and meadows would be washed away by a flood. This kid was Samson. She'd told me about him. And now, he was there, doing exactly what Andrea needed no one to do.

And I felt something I hadn't before, sparked by that one little tear. This was hot and intense and made me cackle without trying to.

And I think it's what made me jump out of Andrea's arm, pull the leash out of her hand and try to bite at his fingers, peck his feet and chase him out of the room, screaming, till he was gone, and then walk calmly back to Andrea to snuggle in peace.

But then again, we can never be sure.

Chapter 16
To Look and To See: 259

That evening, Andrea talked to neither her Mom nor her Dad, she didn't smile, and she didn't look into my eyes.

"How did it go?" Andrea's Mom asked, trying to conceal her excitement.

Andrea shrugged. "Tomorrow."

And the conversation ended.

She put me in the coop, where I, too was bombarded with questions from Lacey and Snowflake, and was happy to relate the tales to my sisters. But Andrea didn't come outside to play with us that night like she typically did.

It wasn't until the next morning that my confusions were put to rest. She sat stroking me, just as the sun lighted the sky into a golden pink, and reflected in her big brown eyes. She got up this time each morning to spend time with us before she ate breakfast and went to school.

"I'm scared to go back." She whispered, just as I settled into the silence, expecting no words from her precious lips. "I want you to come." She sighed heavily and laid her face into my feathers, now thick and full, not scattered with chick fuzz. "When I think it's working, that I'm breaking out of what I am in, it tightens it's grip. I can't just talk. All last night, I couldn't. I don't know what I can't, but I just can't." She paused, forming the words in

83

her head, "I can talk to you, but everyone else, they, they *look* Star. They watch me and won't let me just think."

She looked into my eyes now, and she read my silent language, so similar to hers, "Do you even understand what I'm talking about, Star? You always do." She sighed and looked back to space again as the sun erupted into golden streaks across the sky. Finally her words came out again: "I hate myself. I hate who I am. I wish I could be someone else. Anyone." A scalding tear fell onto my feathers. My heart ached for her all the more. I couldn't keep silent.

"You are amazing, Andrea. And if Samson can't understand that, if you can't understand that, well, then okay, but I do. The way you can see me, no one but you can see past a chicken's eyes. And the way you care. You care about everyone. You're autism isn't the problem..." I stopped, my words coming to a halt, trying to find what I was trying to say, even if she didn't understand, maybe somehow by some miracle these words would cross the species' border and she'd understand. I at least hoped so. **"You are not the problem. They are. Its the world who doesn't see right. There is nothing wrong with you, other than that they've hurt you. The rest of it is just the beautiful valley, though it sees storms, it endures them. That's you, Andrea. And even if the entire world can't see that..."** I nuzzled my face into her cascading hair, **"I still do."**

Andrea looked down at me one time, and gave a hint of a smile, and I knew at least some of the message made it through, as Andrea nodded and stood up to go to school.

Snowflake and Lacey hopped over quietly. **"That was really sweet, Star."** Lacey said softly.

I wasn't at all ashamed that they heard me, in fact, I wished all the world heard me, especially as the usually wild and playful Snowflake said sincerely and gently, **"Star, I see it too."**

+++++++++++

Of course she did go back to school. And better yet, she came home with her small smile adorning her face. She was silently sitting on the cool grass with us, when her Mom came out and sat next to her without a sound. They didn't look at each other, and they didn't speak, but I hopped onto the woman's lap and I felt a new hand stroking my feathers.

"I talked to Penny today." Andrea's quiet, soft words hardly broke the silent afternoon, but sang to its inaudible tune.

Then Mrs. Johnson's eyes met her daughter's with a bright smile. "Someone talked to you?" I could tell she didn't mean to sound so surprised.

Andrea nodded slightly. "She liked Star yesterday."

Her mom's hand stopped on my feathers,

85

and no one said anything for a moment. Finally, she found her voice. "Was she nice to you, Andrea?"

Again, the response was delayed. "Yes. Very." She finally murmured.

"I'm so happy for you Andrea. And really proud of you too."

Andrea scooped me off her moms lap and placed me in her own. "I think...she understands."

I watched Mrs. Johnson smile, then say softly, "I think I understand, too, Andrea."

My friend sighed, and held me a bit tighter. "No, you don't. But...I want you to."

And with that she reverted back to a restful silence.

+++++++++++

The next day, Andrea's Mom did the same thing. Today, however, Susan spoke first. "Did you see Penny today?"

"Yes."

"She's still nice?"

"Yes."

Mrs. Johnson said nothing more, giving Andrea her space.

"Can I go to her birthday party?" Andrea finally said in her short, straight to the point way.

"Well....um, were you invited?" Her mom said with ill-hidden surprise.

"Yes."

"When is it?"

"Tomorrow, 2:00 p.m. Her house is 247 W. Liam Way."

Mrs. Johnson let out a surprised yet

relieved laugh, "Sure, I'll take you. I'd like to meet Penny and her family. I'm really proud of you for being so brave sweetie."

Andrea looked straight into her mom's eyes, surprising us both, "Thanks, Mom."

++++++++++

260

The next day, Andrea skipped over to me her eyes shining happily. She picked me up and spun me around, her hair flying like her spirit, and the world passing in a blur. I nearly fell over when she did put me down. "You're invited too. 'Oh, you don't know how much I love to know that I am loved. When you get a taste of love it can never be enough.'" She sang and said and the same time.

Andrea was excited. She was dancing, smiling, talking excited, to go to a party, whatever that was. I wondered if she'd ever been to a party before. People seemed to talk to her less than she even talked to them. Neither of us understood it, but I guess it was because she was so different. The same reason I saw her as amazing, was the same reason everyone else ran away.

But why not Penny?

I hoped this party might have an answer.

Chapter 17
To Let One In the Walls: 260

My sisters, too, came on this adventure. Last minute, Mrs. Url, Penny's mom, said she would love us to come as a small, all-chicken petting zoo. There was only going to be a few people at this party, anyway. At least, to most people's standards. To Andrea and I, there seemed to be a lot. We were introduced to Penny's cousins, aunts, uncles, parents, grandparents, and three friends along with their families. I mean, Andrea was introduced, most people don't specifically introduce themselves to a chicken, but I was clutched tightly in my owners arms, so I saw it all. We were also introduced to Penny's two siblings, a 6 and a 4-year-old girls who stayed by and clung to Mrs. Url the whole time. Then Penny's three other friends, one girl from school, named Lia, another girl who went to Penny's church, Olivia, who was very nice and talked to Andrea for awhile, though she was several years older, and a boy who was Olivia's brother and walked on shiny legs. Penny said they were....prothstecit or something. He really liked Snowflake, Lacey and I, especially Snowflake. I have to admit, she *is* very likable.

Then there were the cousins, two older girls and one boy. They all towered over poor Andrea, but hardly talked to her. They seemed nice enough, and said nothing mean, but simply smiled shyly at her, as if she were a fragile vase too valuable to be touched.

I was happy to be put down in a small pen with Lacey and Snowflake after hearing so many names and seeing so many faces and trying to make sure Andrea was okay through the whole time. **"We're at a PARTY!"** Snowflake cackled, flapping her wings and running circles. **"Look at all these people! It's. So. Awesome!!!"** She jumped up as high as she could, nearly out of the small pen in the grass. **"People are going to come hold and pet us, and play… we're a *petting zoo*."** She said the last two words slow and careful, trying to say them right.

Lacey nudged me, **"I won't let them drop you, sis."**

I turned to face her, confused for just a moment, **"why would they…?"** A memory came back to me, when I was at the store, and they dropped me, and how scared I'd been for several weeks, even months, afterward.

But that wasn't me. Not anymore. Perhaps I must admit a little fear leaked through the defenses I'd put up against it, but it was quickly quelled and I had my confidence and love.

I laughed. **"That's not going to bother me anymore, Lacey. But thanks. I hadn't even thought of it."** I nuzzled up next to her, **"But I won't let them drop you either."**

Lacey smiled, **"Really? I mean I noticed you didn't seem scared anymore but…"**

"I'm fine. Really." I smiled, focusing on love and not fear, worth and not worry.

"I'm glad." She smiled back.

Snowflake stuck her head between us and looked back and forth, **"Then let's PARTY!!"**

And people came in our little pen, and of course Andrea stayed with us the whole time. Mrs. Johnson made sure we were safe and comfortable. Penny hugged each one of us with a huge smile, and yet a perfectly gentle hand. She talked to us like we were her friends, as though she knew us like Andrea did. The other kids petted us gently, or maybe picked us up. A few decided not to come in at all. Everyone was kind, however, and we all enjoyed it. When it was time for other games, cake and presents, I left the pen and sat in my spot: Andrea's arms.

When Penny opened one particular box, wrapped absolutely perfectly in gray wrapping paper with a drawing of a chicken on the side, and I recognized that it was Andrea's gift to her new friend. A hushed confusion settled over the group as it was opened. It was just blocks. A handful of toy blocks. Andrea's blocks. They were tied together neatly with sting and had a small tag, also with a drawing of a chicken, and the words were somewhat of a clear and obvious to me, like a straight-forward riddle.

To Penny: you get me like no one else ever has. You are like a chicken. And so you are invited to build my city. You are in my city. -Andrea Johnson.

91

She had the cleanest handwriting, and to me it made sense, Penny, however, would have to wait until she came to our house, then she'd see. But for now, she had 8 blocks, tied together painted in a shiny copper tone, the color of Penny's hair, and the color of a penny. Andrea was going to put Penny in her city.

Andrea Johnson
Chapter 18
Building the City: 268

I couldn't tell you when the change exactly happened. But now, in a way, I liked myself. I looked in the mirror, and saw amber eyes, glossy brown and wavy hair, a tall, ten year old girl, who claimed to be myself. And I liked her. And yet, it was more than what I looked like that I began to look at with pleasure instead of shame. As the tide drawing back with every wave into low tide in the afternoon, no one could tell you when that switch happened, but when you see the line of once-wet sand, you see it clearly. Sometimes we judge the world, judge ourselves, and take it all in, by where we've been. And that's when you see where you're going. I wasn't disgusted by the word 'autism'. I didn't push it away so hard, and then, it stopped pushing back.

When a hand brushed mine it still shocked me inside to out. When I walked through a hall of loud students, my ears still felt like bursting. I still preferred to be quiet over talking. Okay, so maybe I hadn't changed at all. That was exactly what made the change so radical. I didn't hate myself anymore. Maybe autism wasn't a curse. I decided to be who I was. And I guess it was Star who showed me the way. I had changed, yet I was who I always had been. I'd always been looking away, and now I looked out, and saw beautiful things. It was wonderful. But nothing lasts forever.

+++++++++++

Penny was coming over to help build my city. To build herself. We were waiting for her, Star sat in the house with me, and we watched TV, except neither of us were actually watching it. Her and I were the only two who'd built the city. And now, I chose to let Penny in. I hoped she wouldn't knock it down. No one tried to, I don't think. It's like when they tap my shoulder, and a whirlpool of feelings overwhelm me. Or when they walk by with the laundry, and a piece of clothing falls on the blocks, destroying the city.

But I don't know about Penny. She likes chickens. She is like a chicken. Never seeming to judge, never seeming to question, just know. Her presence like a wisp, gentle, not harming, caring, yet mysterious and funny. A wisp of vapor cannot harm it city. But a vapor comes from an ocean. And an ocean is harmful. I'm scared of the oceans. The ones in my mind, at least. There *are* the gentle ripples that give me more emotions I do not understand, though I like them. The oceans, though, the big waves, the real ones that are twenty minutes away from our house. They scare me. That's something I understand: fear. No, I don't mean *I'm scared of the dark*. Or *"Yikes, you scared me."*

Scary as in my heart quakes, my legs

go numb, my tongue can't be found in my own mouth, my own mind flies out the back window and leaves me in utter darkness. I can't move, can't speak, can't think, can't. Just *can't.* That's when I find a wall, when I start to feel the oceans and I flick it away, the most useless and desperate attempt but all I know to do. When it takes over me, I scream, I cry, I push and shove and refuse everything. That's fear to me. And its almost what I felt when I heard the knock on the door. Almost.

Star nudged me, I stood, I greeted the smiling figure at the door. Her bright eyes, and all.

"Hi Andrea! Hi, Star! How are you?"

I managed a smile, but I knew it didn't look right. I couldn't get words out of my mouth yet. So we just showed her to my room. Star hopped out of my arms and began her usual excited routine: floor, bed, desk, floor. Penny laughed. I liked it, her laugh like the prettiest song anyone could ever write. "Woah..." Penny's song-voice came through when her eyes met the city. "You built *all this?*"

I finally found my tongue: "Yeah."

She walked over and with one long, white finger brushed across the wooden blocks, not disturbing a single one. "What...I mean...like, why? How long have you been...?" It was amusing to see someone else losing their words, and the fear withdrew slightly.

"4 years." I answered her unfinished question. It took me longer to consider her first incomplete question: *why?* She helped me, though, as she pointed out miniature wooden-block landmarks.

"What is this?" She would say, pointing to a gray building, mostly fallen over.

"My old school." I'd reply. She looked at me and smiled, understanding how this would work.

"And this?" Motioning to the tall, long blocks in the very center of the city, shaped as a little *t*.

"Jesus." Was my happy answer. No one had ever asked me about my city before. But then again, I'm not sure I ever would have answered. We went at this for awhile, me telling of each member of my family, the building that represented color and the one for numbers, and one for reading. Then she came to the three statues close to the middle, but just off to the right. Penny smiled and didn't even ask what they were, seeing the obvious chicken shapes. Star strutted over to hers and cackled at it, then she walked over to me and hopped on my lap, it would turn out to be a good thing too, because Penny came to a tall building, a green and brown tower. It was leaning over considerably, and about to fall. And if it did fall, it would crush the entire city by the angle of it. Penny frowned when she looked at it, but made no move to touch it. "What is this…?"

I held tight onto Star, and bit my lip. Why was it so hard to explain? "My brother." I finally whispered.

"I didn't know you had a brother." Penny

said sadly.

"I never see him." It hurt to think about. I'd been trying not to, because it just made the tower lean more. It was the one thing that kept me hating myself, and wanting to just be a normal little girl: Charlie. I wanted Charlie to come home.

I also wanted to tell someone, which was something I'd never felt before. And so I stroked Star's back soothingly, for her and me, and slowly started to explain in the best way I could:

"He's 10 years older than me. I was 7 when my autism was really bad. Mom and Dad tried to figure out what to do. They took me to therapy more. They sent me to a private school, two years late, and read books, went to speeches, they did everything. Charlie thought I should just stay home and he'd help me, and Mom and Dad. He tried really hard to understand me, and helped be so much just by, by being my big brother. But he was wrong. I needed JoAnn Carol to do my therapy with me. But he thought he was helping. Eventually they got so mad, Charlie said he'd leave when he was 18, instead of watch them hurt me." I sighed, and realized I was squeezing Star, and let go. She stayed with me anyways. "He left. And it hurt me more than anything. Now I'm scared of myself. All I ever do is hurt people." I closed my eyes and shook my head, trying to get rid of it all. "I'm sorry. I-I didn't mean to..." Then something amazing happened, Penny hugged me. But not the fierce, shocking way people usually touched me. She scooted next to me, leaned her shoulder on mine, but one arm around me ever so gently, and the other, and laid her head down. *This*, I thought, *is what a hug is supposed to feel like.* And so I wrapped my arms around her.

When she lifted her head, she smiled, though her eyes were filled with oceans, more literal than mine. "I've never heard you talk so much, Andrea."

I smiled slightly and sighed, "I've been planning on saying that for 2 and a half years. I just never had anyone to say it to."

Star hopped onto Penny's lap and nudged her, giving the thank you I wasn't sure how.

"You came to build this city." I said, pointing to the blocks "but you built this one even more." And I pointed to my heart.

Chapter 19
The Rising Tides: 271

I guess I can hear things equally. *All* things. At a restaurant, if I ever go, I can hear the conversations at each table on the same level. It's overwhelming, and it can really be a problem. This one day, it was a serious problem. Star, Lacey, Snowflake and I were inside playing. I was trying to get them used to the chicken diapers. My room is right just down the hall from the kitchen, and I heard Mom and Dad talking. And Mom, she was crying.

"Mike, we can't. You know we *can't*. It's not even an option. Do they realize just what they're asking from us?"

"No, they don't. But it'll be okay, Honey." Dad reassured her. I tried not to listen. It didn't work.

"Okay?! How could it be okay? You know we can't just comply."

"I know, and I'm not planning on it. We can go to the city council next week, okay? We'll get this figured out. And Charlie's offered to help."

"Charlie?! He hasn't talked to us in months! How does he even know about it?"

"He called, asking about Andrea. He misses her. She was at school, so she couldn't talk to him, but he wanted to hear all about her. I told him about the chickens, and the complaints. He got into law school, you know. He could really help us."

Charlie called?! My mind started to race.

"He's only 21! And we haven't talked in almost 3 years! And *he* wants to help *us?*"

"He's the one who's offered. And you know he's in law school, he could really help. And you know as well as I do that we can't let pride get in the way." Then he mumbled, "and maybe we can get our son back too." I was about to run out and ask if I could call Charlie back, then Dad kept talking: "Andrea needs the chickens. And we won't give up until this is sorted out."

"And what if we can't convince the Council?"

"The letter specifically warns that without compliance they will confiscate them."

"What's the date we have to comply before?" Mom's voice was already shaking.

"A month from today."

Another sob escaped from my mom.

"It's okay, Susan. It's okay." Dad's voice went to a whisper. And I slid against the wall and let my tears flow freely. I was causing problems again. Big problems, that made even Mom cry. And "they" wanted to confiscate my chickens.

I'm just glad I didn't know what confiscation was.

+++++++++++
280

I turned away from the kid at school, pretending he wasn't there. But he was, and I wished he'd leave already. He was trying to catch up with me, for some reason. And he wasn't Samson. His name was Marcus. He'd never talked to me before, but I knew what his name was, and I knew he talked to Samson. Again, the hearing thing. Finally, he tapped me on the shoulder, sending me against the wall with a gasp at the sudden contact.

"What's the deal?" He put his hands up dramatically, as if I were overreacting. *Am I?* I thought to myself and kept walking, still pretending he wasn't talking to me. I could hardly hear him over everyone else, anyway, it was all so loud in my head.

"I'm talking to you." He jumped in front of me so I had to stop. I couldn't look in his deep, blue eyes, so I looked at his yellow shoes.

"'There are some things that no matter how long, or how much or how well you describe, no one can understand.' -Oliver Breadwell." Something gentler washed over his eyes, when I finally glanced at them, but I looked back down, as I saw another boy and a girl walking over. This boy coming over was Samson. "She causing you trouble, Marcus?" He asked with a sneer in his voice. It made me shudder.

"No, Sams-" He started with a stutter.

"I liked whatcha said about her little act, Marcus. Its so true, and somebody's gotta speak up 'bout it." The girl chimed in with a sassy tone.

"What? What'd ya say? I wasn't by you in class, didn't hear you." Samson added.

"He kept all quiet 'bout it like a genius, just so a few people could hear him, but not the whole class, and not teacher." The girl smirked.

"Just tell me, stupid." Samson demanded, as I slid harder and harder against the wall. I really wished they'd stop. I had heard what Marcus had said, and I wished I didn't have to hear it again.

"When Mrs. Peterson said that everyone did a good job on their show and tells, Marcus says 'everyone but Andrea and her silly act with an illegal chicken? And she's got no more talent than a sunflower.'"

"I didn't say *all* that—"

"Dude! That true? The bird's illegal?"

Both kids looked at Marcus, who looked about as shy and out of place as me. Well, no, not quite.

"Um, yeah. My dad said they have to get rid of them. There's no livestock allowed in La Mesa."

"What if they don't get rid of them?"

"Um... they'll take them away."

I wished I could disappear, but they had me cornered. I needed Star right now.

But my heart leaped into my throat, tears sprang to my eyes. They said other things as well, but I wanted nothing more than to be gone. Completely gone. I'd heard Mom say it. Confiscate=take. Illegal birds=my chickens. I sat down on the floor. And covered my face with my hands, shaking my head until I couldn't hear the voices clearly. I didn't stop until they went away, and a hand gently took mine and pulled me up from the ground. It was just Marcus now, the other kids were gone. He bent to look in my eye. I hated him for it. He even pushed my hair out of the way to see me. "Hey, you okay?" He smiled a little. I nodded a little, though I knew it was a lie. He wrapped his arms around himself.

"I-I actually came over to tell you I'm sorry. I mean, I don't know if you understand me or not, because you're so weird, but I mean, your show and tell was actually good. And, I mean" He sighed and ran his hand through his light brown hair. "I probably look stupid, apologizing to a disabled kid, but I, I guess I mean it. Maybe you could try to be more normal, and we all wouldn't be so mean? I don't know. Just forget it. I'm sorry, anyway. And I hope I didn't upset you by what I said with they chickens. I really wish it weren't that way. You aren't even listening, are you? Do you even know what I'm saying?"

I shook my head. I didn't *want* to understand.

"I didn't think so. I'm not wasting my time."

He started to walk away, and it was only after a few steps that he paused. "Hang on a second, if you answered me…" He turned around. But by time, I was already gone.

Star
Chapter 20
Worth the Fight: 280

I really didn't know what was happening. All I knew was that Andrea ran to me after school and cried into my feathers. But it was different from how she normally came to me.

It wasn't like she was overwhelmed or confused. It was like all the ocean was still, but storm clouds hung overhead. No crashing waves in her eyes. But no excited sparks or splashes. The storm on the distant horizon: gray, solid, dull, and dark, rain pattering on the gray surface and wind howling silently. That was Andrea today.

She whispered that she didn't want me to leave. That I couldn't leave.

"I'm *not* going to leave you, Andrea. I would never want to leave. I'll stay right here in your arms, forever and always." I tried to comfort her. When she left, with hunched shoulders and red in her usually-bright eyes, I noticed that even bright Snowflake had the same stormy look. And worse, Lacey did too. **"Guys, what's the matter? I'm really not going anywhere. I promise."**

Snowflake turned quickly to cry in a nesting box without a word. Something was *very* wrong. **"Lacey, at least explain to me what is happening."** I begged her, feeling time had stopped and left me behind.

"It was the other day, when you were inside, and Mr. and Mrs. Johnson came outside to talk—without Andrea listening." She paced in a circle, thinking hard, before continuing. "We're not supposed to be here. And someone is going to try to take us away. They're going to try to get whoever it is to change their mind, but..." she sighed and shook her head, leaving the rest unfinished.

Time did stop then, I closed my eyes and forced myself to keep on breathing. I had to say something, I had to not say something, because then I'd know it wasn't a dream, I tried to calm myself and words finally found themselves. "It... it can't be true. I'm not leaving. I'm not. And neither are you, or any of us. We've got to stay together. You know that! With Andrea...and...and...I really don't want anything to change... and... and it's all going to be OK." I took a deep breath. "It's got to be okay." I shook my head, "Remember, Lacey, when we were little, you told me we'd be okay. That the food always came, that...that we'd be okay..."

"I know I did, Star. And maybe sometimes our idea of okay is different from the real okay."

Tears started to fall from my eyes "I don't know what you mean, Lacey."

"I mean we might think we need the food now, but there's still some in the feeder. When we really need it, that's when God will give it to us."

"You're not just talking about food, are you?"

"No. I mean we think we need to stay here and it's what we know, we need Andrea and she needs us but if we have to go apart... He knows what we need and when we need it."

"But I still...I just don't want to lose her." I closed my eyes.

"It's not up to us, Star."

"I know. Because we're *just chickens*."

++++++++++
283

I hated the weather. It was beautiful. The sun shone, the birds sang, the grass was wet and dewy. It contradicted all of me.

The family ate lunch outside when it was this nice out. And today there was another person.

He was tall and had sandy colored hair. His smile was too bright for my dark mind, but his eyes, they looked like Andrea's.

And Andrea doesn't hug people. But she hugged him. She didn't let go of him. Her eyes sparked and swam at the same time, all with the dark cloud still lingering behind. He sat down at the little outside-table, and my friend finally left his side for more than a moment to open up our coop. She scooped me up and took me to him.

"Is this Star?" He asked, reaching to pet my back. She nodded and stroked me as well. "We'll take care of her, okay sis?" He looked at

Andrea lovingly.

She nodded again and whispered, "Thanks, Charlie." That's when I understood who this person was. It was Andrea's brother. No wonder Andrea's face beamed. Then there was technical just talk I didn't understand:

"So, the three of us will go to the council tomorrow. Do you both have your points written out?" Charlie would say, acting businesslike.

"Yes." Andrea's Dad would answer.

"Charlie, you know you really don't have to do all this…"

"It's okay, Mom. I…I really want to."

"But we're only allowed to speak at the public speech time, right?"

"Yeah, but that's not what it's called…" And so they drawled on, and all I got was that they were trying to change the minds of whoever wanted to take us away. But it wasn't going to be easy. It didn't loosen my tension. I rubbed my beak on Andrea's cheek as the adults discussed. She gently rubbed me back. "'We're gonna be alright, going to be alright.'" Her voice was a whisper. I wasn't sure if she was telling herself or me.

+++++++++++
284

"If you had anyone supporting you, then we could consider. Your argument is valid and I understand that your chickens are not livestock, they are pets, but the fact is, neighbors are complaining. And if they repealed and said they wanted you to keep the chickens, then that would be perfectly fine. We can't repeal the confiscation because you reject it. That doesn't change the reason it was issued in the first place.

"Show us the support that they are not "livestock" and that everyone is alright with them in the city, and the issue will be almost immediately solved. But if you are the only ones who are supporting yourself, well, no matter how strong a table is it cannot hold itself up. You cannot only have your own support. If you cannot show the support, as you so far have not, you may not keep the chickens, and they will be transported to the San Diego Humane Society until we decide what to do with them. I am sorry. But it is what is going to happen."

"Sir, you don't understand—" Charlie had stood up to argue. "They aren't any more loud or smelly than a dog...why, if you just saw Andrea and what they mean to her..."

"I'm sorry, but that's not what this is about. It's just beside the point."

"So all you care about is whether or not it's the law? Not people? Their lives? Just the law? Just if your paycheck comes in and you make the next election?!..."

"Sir, please sit down. I am sorry. But it's just what we have to do..." Even the City Council member couldn't argue Charlie's point, but dodged the bullet narrowly.

"I'm not sitting down. I'm making my point: you say it has to be the neighbors who repeal their complaint? That we have to prove the city's support?"

"Yes." The Council member was clearly done with the subject.

"Then I propose a solution."

"You are not on the Council. You cannot propose bills."

" Not a bill. A contest."

"You sound like a child."

"I have the determination of a child, if that's what it takes. So let's say, we prove we have the support of the city, you'll drop it all? The chickens stay?"

"Well," the man hesitated, "yes. I don't have a problem with the chickens personally, I guess they aren't technically illegal in and of themselves but merely causing issues on a city wide level and causing complaints. So if you prove those are not issues, yes, there will be no problem, I should say."

"Then at the next council, if we can bring in a signed petition, to keep the chickens, we'll be good? Andrea can keep them?"

"Well, I mean…if you have the support, because we represent the people and if it proves that it is their opinion…"

"Just yes or no." Charlie's voice was taut.

The council member discussed it with the other members for a while.

"Yes." and he said under his breath "It's not typical, but we aren't getting anywhere

andrea Johnson

until we do something." Then he turned to them all. "Bring the support and the chickens stay. Two hundred signatures."

"Done." Charlie smiled, while his parents sat flabbergasted.

I heard this all from Andrea. I'd never heard her talk so much at once. But apparently it'd been third-hand quoted. Charlie was talking most of it, and Andrea's Mom had told it for Andrea, word for word, and she told it to me. It was nice to hear her talk. But the words shook my world loose again, as it rattled back and forth on a point. One side was peace and rest, continued life at home, with my family, with *Andrea*.

On the other side was a deep abyss with unknowns at the bottom. The only certainty was that there: Andrea would not be with me.

Chapter 21
Within Our Walls: 285

It was so different. Penny came over. That was not different. She walked into the backyard, and to the coop, where Andrea was stroking us. Penny smiled sadly, looking back and forth from Andrea to the ground, not sure what to say. Andrea walked out of the coop, and the two hugged each other. That was different. But that was certainly not the only thing that had changed in Andrea recently. Her eyes lit up more, she told us more about school. But now, what we were facing together was an earthquake. It shook the whole ground. It left the skies clear and blue, only with clouds on the horizon, and the beauty remained untouched, but the quaking threatened to destroy it all, without a word. I savored the perfect beauty with all the bravery I could muster.

"So...how's the city?" Penny finally asked, softly breaking the long silence, us now sitting under a tree with my chicken family and me.

Andrea swallowed hard and clicked her tongue a few times. "'I'm not sure what will stand.' John Calmo."

Penny frowned, and reached for Andrea's hand. But this time Andrea yanked it away, and stared at the ground. I looked up at Penny, and a spark came to her eye. She reached into her pocket and pulled out a pad of paper and pen. She scribbled for a few moments before giving it to Andrea.

"I'm really sorry about them trying to take away your chickens. You know my family will offer our support. And…I will offer mine, to you, right now."

Andrea's eyes scanned the paper, and then they flew to Penny's with a now-rare splash in them. Her lips turned up slightly, and she snatched the pen.

"This is going to be the only way I can talk right now. Sorry." It took her several minutes before she handed it to her friend.

"You have no reason to be sorry. I love you, whether you talk or not. Your difficulty sharing what is inside doesn't mean there's nothing there. And you can share it now, if you want."

"How did you know to do this?"

"I thought writing might be easier." Penny's simple replies came quickly, Andrea fiddled with each word for minutes, but I marveled at the silent communication happening between the friends. I snatched the note from penny's hand and carried it to Andrea, bringing the fulfilling sound of laughter to my ears. But Andrea frowned when she saw the note.

"That's not what I meant. How did you know… how to deal with me? How'd you see through me?"

Penny bit her lip as she read it, and when I carried it back, it had one wet teardrop that smeared the ink. *"We're all different, Andrea. It doesn't take a rocket surgeon to be kind."* Then she added on the bottom, *"And I always liked your chickens."* And *Andrea* reached for Penny's hand, and I sat on top of them both.

+++++++++++

287

An all too familiar sound was coming from the nest boxes. Lacey was out playing with Andrea, and Snowflake was no where in sight, so I went to find her again, and when I hopped up onto the perch I frowned and tears stung my eyes once more.

"Snowflake," I whispered, **"Don't cry."** It was no use of course, and my heart broke as her big, blue eyes turned on me, and her soft fuzz on her face wet with tears.

"Why...why wouldn't I cry?" She sniffled. I nuzzled in next to her.

I thought about her question for a moment. It struck me hard. I couldn't say that I hadn't cried in the past few days. Couldn't say I didn't want to cry right now. But Snowflake shouldn't have to worry about it, she should know that... that was it, I knew what to say now.

"Andrea doesn't want you to be sad, Snowflake."

"Why does she still care? We can't stay with her."

My heart broke all over again, **"Because...you don't...you don't have to be with someone, or understand them, or know what they're thinking...to love them. And**

love matters more than any of that."

She sniffled and sat still for a minute.
"But I'm scared."

It brought back a flood of memories:
fear. I thought about how scared I was, and
Snowflake helping me, in her own little way.
Now, if ever, was the time to be scared. Very
scared. Why wasn't I so helplessly scared
anymore? I was scared, scared of that day
Andrea would be pried away forever, but I
had something other than fear. I strained my
thoughts to remember. It had flowed through
my thoughts every day since then, and kept
that fear away. Like a lantern, constantly
chasing the darkness away. It was such a part
of me now that I nearly forgot what it was.
Bravery. That was it. But how to be brave? A
light in the darkness, God made us all, we are
all bad... what was the good? There was good
somewhere. That puzzle piece, that link, that
one thing that held it all together. What made
the light shine? What made the fear leave?
What made God make us good? The questions
ran through my mind and the answer pulled
itself just out of reach until I felt it as I looked
in my sister's eyes. God was good, God loved,
yes, then I knew it. *Love.* And love is enough
to make anyone brave. The pieces fit perfectly,
and I smiled contentedly, though solemnly. **"I
used to be scared a lot, Snowflake."** I started,
looking across the yard at the blossoming
flowers. **"Scared of everything. And...and
you know how I got over it? What made it**

go away?" She shook her head but searched my eyes. **"Love. I love you, and Lacey, and Andrea, and…God, too much to be scared of anything. Even…"** I swallowed hard, deciding if I could handle these words: **"Even if I have to lose them. Because I know that we'll all be okay. That God will always keep me safe, and keep you safe and Lacey and even when I can't see it, Andrea too. So even if everything goes wrong. Because we are loved. And love is enough to make us brave."** Snowflake shoved her beak against me for a few moments.

"Thank you, Star." She finally said before we went back to playing, to enjoy our time, however long it may be, and love. No matter what, we were going to love.

+++++++++++
290

It was just Andrea and me in the bright, cool room. We were building the city. And that alone made my heart swell. *The city was still being built,* even when the whole world seemed to be crashing. But the city had always had a wall. It was a tall wall that was a perfect square all the way around the city. For the past few weeks, each day I came in, I watched her continue to take it down. Today, she took down the last block, and smiled at me. She rubbed my head and hugged me. "We did it, Star." She whispered. Then she picked up the block she'd just removed, sat at a small table, and coated

117

it with a rose-colored paint, setting it down carefully. I cocked my head at her peculiar actions. What was she doing? Next she pulled out a box from her drawer, and dumped out a pile of blocks of the same color. It was the wall she'd been taking down. Andrea took them each carefully, and began turning them around and building them into shapes on the ground, lining them up, around the buildings, back out, to the farthest edges of her old school around the innermost buildings of me, and her mom, and to the very center, the cross. I wasn't sure I'd ever seen her so enthusiastic. But why? Why when the world was falling apart? I followed her around and she petted and hugged me every once in awhile, sometimes singing a song or two. When she was at last done, the process taking long enough that the last block was dry, and she slid it into the open space, but left it sticking out, and set me in front of it. I looked at the block, and back to her, back to the block. I pushed it in with my beak. The new wall was done. Andrea picked me up, so I could look down on the art piece. The rose-colored outline looked somewhat like a flower, petals folding over onto themselves, some larger and some smaller, but all of them around the buildings, in a chaotic but graceful and cohesive masterpiece.

"Thank you, Star." Her hushed voice met my ears as I stared at the beautiful reflection of this beautiful girl's feelings, her voice unraveling her own riddle. "I've learned to like

my wall, and help people into it. All because
God used you." She stopped and sighed. "It's
still hard. And...I don't want you to leave. But
somehow...I think it'll be okay. Because... I'll still
love you. Even if you're not there, I *will* be brave."

I looked away from the city and into her
bright brown eyes, **"Andrea, I will be brave too."**

Chapter 22
I'll Still Be Brave: 299

Words will never tell, memory will never grasp, and imagination will never begin to satisfy the truth of that day. It'd been several weeks since we'd heard we might be leaving, so we tried to let ourselves forget and have a false hope I guess. Maybe it was silly of us, but we couldn't take it any other way. I slid across the metal crate, it reminding me of the day that Andrea took us home. It brought a fresh supply of tears to my eyes. *Home*. What *was* our home. Now, it wasn't. In my heart it still was, always would be, but it was not. Now, we were in the back of a pickup truck, driving away from my Andrea. I closed my eyes and saw her in my mind again, standing straight, waving her hands bravely, but I saw through her ocean-filled, amber eyes, she was falling inside. The storm hit and the earthquake was rattling apart her world. It was shaking mine to pieces, too. And I wasn't there to help her through it, and she wasn't there to help me.

"We've gotta be brave, Star. Love alone is worth it to fight. The Lord our God will be with us wherever we go." She'd whispered to me, and I quaked when I realized it was the last, sweet whisper I'd ever hear her say. And the piece of my heart that was still a fragment of whole, now it broke. Now we bounced along, the wind

stealing our breath, the wind of time stealing our time, stealing hope, and love. And in the back of a pickup truck, in one metal kennel, sliding against one another like we were chicks again. Maybe it was the start of a new life, I attempted to stir the fire of hope within me again. To let the cool waters splash gently instead of crashing and drowning me and tearing me apart. But if that hope ever grew, it dissipated quickly. I didn't want a new life. I didn't want to be brave anymore. I looked back again, back to the place Andrea was waving bravely only a few minutes ago. Nothing but an empty road behind. Nothing but an empty road ahead. And the last shimmer of hope blew away into the wind.

+++++++++++

"She's really gone, Star." Even Lacey sounded hopeless. We were sitting in an office, a strange place for chickens, but they had no other place for us at the moment. I turned to the red chicken, her deep, dark eyes sad and shining.

A nod was all I could manage. Thoughts were racing around my head. *"Even if you're not here, I'll be brave."* Andrea's precious words echoed through my head. She was being brave. She'd stood up and waved, she hadn't hid and broken down, like I was doing inside. *"I'll still always love you."* She'd said, so firm and true. I looked at my sisters, down-cast and broken, like me. *Why be brave? Why keep loving when I'll never see you again?* She had said that God loves us all. Why? Why did Andrea love?

Why should I? Without the answer it'd all fall apart. It was easy enough to say "I love you" but what about when it was this hard? What is love? The food had run out, and no one was refilling it. We tried to make it to the horizon but the storms had overtaken us.

And I looked at Snowflake and Lacey. They were still near me. I closed my eyes, and thought about Andrea, and she was far away, so far away. *She liked her wall,* she loved who she was. But I was still just a chicken. *Just?* I was a chicken and Andrea said God used me. He used chickens! I mattered to Him! Andrea mattered to Him! Snowflake, Lacey, Penny, even Samson? They did too? Yes. And they mattered to me to. Love is bravery. Love is passion, care, strength, and weakness sometimes too. And she knew what love was, and she felt it, for me. And now I felt it for them too. All of them. And so I'd be brave. I'd keep loving because it love was beautiful and I'd rather love and say goodbye than to have stayed in that lonely world I was in when I was little. God gave me that food, and I needed it now, and He gave me Lacey and Snowflake, no one had forgotten. I'd needed Andrea then, I still needed her in a way, but it was going to be okay, because this was worth it to have done *anything.* Much more to have made it so far as we did, and who knew what would happen next, it was terrifying, but I wasn't afraid anymore. God would never stop loving, and neither would I. Andrea loved because she knew it, I would love because she taught me.

"Andrea wanted us to be brave." I said in a hushed voice at last. My sisters looked at me. "She learned to love herself, even if she is different. And...we can love what was, and hope for what will be, because she loves us, God loves us, and..." I put my wings around them both, "And I love you." I looked up, and felt a wave of peace amid my broken heart. "I'll still be brave."

Andrea Johnson

I had watched my chickens leave through oceans. They washed over me, tossing my hair across my face, stealing my breath, throwing me around and around until I didn't know which way was the sky.

I'd only been to the actual ocean once. I hated the sand. It clung to me like a thousand needles, but the water was different. It washed over me fears. It took the sand away. It was cold, startling but also soothing.

Then it got too strong and took me, washed over me, tossing my hair across my face, stealing my breath, tossing me around and around until I didn't know which way was the sky. I had never gone back again.

A jolt brought me to the surface of my mind. It was the wind that was blowing my hair, not the ocean. And tears on my face were the waters. Mom was touching my arm, now putting her hand in mine.

The truck was gone. I knew it was gone. I'd seen it leave through the waters, but a piece of me had hoped I saw wrong. But it was gone.

All my bravery left. Everything I'd tried, and thought, and hoped for, it washed away like a wind. Everything Star had done. I let my hand fall away from my mom's, and let more tears fall. I couldn't flick my fingers. I couldn't click my tongue. I couldn't flap my arms. Nothing would chase this feeling away. This, I realized, was sadness.

I couldn't go back. I had to feel this. In a way, it was okay. It was a feeling, a feeling I understood, I could almost feel it, the shape and size of it, and I *knew why it was there*. And, I knew, Star was feeling it too.

I looked at Mom, her brown eyes like mine, filled with oceans, meeting mine. Why did Dad have to not be home today?

"Let's go inside, honey." Her voice was gentle, a smooth and light breeze about the shaking ground and crashing storm. Carefully, I wrapped my arms under hers, softly laid my head upon her strong self. Something that could hold me up, that would not shock me, hurt me, and turn away. I hugged her for one long, precious moment. And then we went inside.

+++++++++++

"We haven't lost hope yet." Dad was saying later once he was home. I was staring at my dinner, not eating it. It'd only been two

125

hours, and I needed my chickens. But I opened up my thoughts enough to listen to what he said.

"We can still try to get that support the Council says we need."

Charlie was there, sitting next to me, trying desperately to comfort me. I felt sorry that it wasn't really working. Of course I loved that he was there, I just…couldn't. Not now.

He spoke up. "I'm arranging a get-together Saturday for support. We're advertising like crazy, Mom. I'm really hopeful."

"'I'll still be alone in this broken world, because only God knows my heart.' -Lloyd Harrison." I murmured quietly, yet apparently loud enough that everyone looked at me.

Charlie looked at me, and gently touched my hand. "You aren't alone, Sis. Not with me you aren't."

He looked back at Mom and Dad. "Does that sound good, guys? Saturday?"

"I'm willing to try anything, at this point." Mom said. Dad just chewed his lip.

Charlie sighed slowly, running his hand over his face. "Dad, Mom," He reached out to pet my long hair softly, "Sis, I'm…I'm sorry. I'm sorry that I tore our family apart just because I was too stubborn listen. And look at you now, Andrea, you're so more than I could have imagined you'd become. And it sounds like part of what helped you was your chickens, and I want to get them back to you." He sighed again, "I want to make up what… what I broke." He cast down his eyes, but I met them. Deep brown against his light hair. Yes — there were oceans in them too. The oceans you could see, not just feel.

"It's okay, Charlie." His teary eyes met mine. "You didn't break me. I — I'm not broken."

His lip quivered, and he smiled. "No you're not, Andrea. And I don't think you ever were."

"Besides," I looked around at my family and then looked down, "We're all just beautifully broken together." I hugged onto Charlie gently. "I forgive you."

Star
Chapter 23
The Outside View: 301

They finally took us outside, into the crisp morning air, and I filled my lungs with a deep breath. But quickly I whipped my head back to what I'd just seen. There — was it? Light brown, wavy hair, dancing legs and twinkling brown eyes. Yes, it was Andrea! Just to see her one more time make me sing inside, and I quickly pointed her out to my sister's beside me. There were other people, too, crowding the courtyard-like area. Mom, Dad, Charlie, Penny, a few other people too. In a flash, Andrea's eyes met mine and lit up as she ran to the cage, setting on a small table now.

"Star!" She gasped. "Oh, Star, Lacey, Snowflake. 'I've been alone in this broken world because only God knows my heart.' -Lloyd Harrison. 'There is a hope, in this dark night.' -Polly Isabelle. 'I'm arranging a get together on Saturday for support… we haven't lost hope yet.' -Charlie Johnson." She smiled a little, and I got her point. This was our last chance. She stuck her finger through the bars, and a rubbed my face against it. "'It's okay, it's okay. Just hold on, my runaway.' - Set Free."

And she got up to leave. She had to. They were making preparations, setting up papers, and making it get people's attention. This was our last chance. We could do it. We had to. A splash had risen inside of me that I hadn't known since Andrea was gone: Happiness.

"Come on, guys, we gotta lighten up. This is our last chance to go back home." I told Snowflake and Lacey.

"You really think, Star? REALLY? We might go *home*?!" Snowflake exploded. I turned to listen to the happenings around me. **"I hope so, Snowflake. And all we can do is hope now."**

+++++++++++

It seemed like a lifetime, sitting there, my nerves racked up and helpless to do anything. But eventually a small crowd gathered, the sun beating down on our shoulders now, shaking off the cold edge of the air. And Charlie stood on the steps of the building we'd come out of, and raised his voice so that all could hear him.

"Um…hello," He cleared his throat. "HELLO, everyone." Finally the many pairs of eyes met his, and he smiled before continuing. "Thank you for being here everybody. I am Charlie Johnson. I think y'all know that we're here to gather enough support for my little sister to keep her chickens. I believe that there must be enough kind, pure-hearted people here who will help us."

I smiled silently as more people who walked by gathered and began to listen.

"Chickens are in fact no louder, or smellier than a dog. They are amazing animals and don't deserve to be treated like they can only be farm animals. Just because they aren't 'normal' pets doesn't mean they shouldn't be pets at all.

They are very personable, can be trained,

and even these chickens here walk on leashes."
He motioned towards us. The crowd just looked
bored.

"Besides this, these chickens are not
livestock. They are *just simply pets*. Besides, there
is a technical difference of what small stock is,
and the city doesn't restrict small stock. Small
stock includes rabbits, chinchillas, ducks, and
yes, even *guinea pigs*. So if anyone in this whole
city has a guinea pig, shouldn't it be confiscated,
too?" Now he was making a point, people started
to catch on. Maybe this would work.

"My sister keeps her coop amazingly
spotless, she spends hours a day with her birds,
keeping them from being too loud, and indeed,
they are less bothersome than neighborhood cats.

So if you'd please," he pulled out a
clipboard "please sign our petition to let the
chickens stay." He handed it to the nearest
person. Charlie had this down, we just had to get
them to sign it. *Right?*

And then the school buses pulled up.

Kids poured out. Angry teachers poured
out. This was bad. There was Samson.

"She…brought…the chicken…to school!"
A round little woman shouted, angrily. "My
daughter is allergic to birds! What were you
thinking?!"

Charlie sputtered out a confused reply,
"Well, um, I'm sorry. But I mean… Andrea…
didn't know that."

"It's just not right to have a girl prance
around with a critter like that, making people feel

sorry, saying it helps them with their 'disability'."
She snorted.

"The chickens have helped Andrea
considerably. She suffers from ASD—"

"Autism is just an excuse for bratty kids to
be bratty." She huffed. Charlie turned red, and
bit his lip to keep himself from shouting.

"Perhaps if you understood—" Penny's
small voice came out of the crowd, but no one
acknowledged her. Mrs. Johnson stood with one
hand over her mouth and the other in Andrea's
hand gently. Charlie, flustered and angry, hopped
down and Mr. Johnson came up.

"Please, listen..." He said loudly, trying to
hush the now large and arguing crowd. Andrea
clicked her tongue and closed her eyes. I watched
it all from the cage, my eyes darting this way and
that to make sense of it all.

"I am Mike Johnson." He announced with
a calm air, "as Charlie said earlier—perhaps
you were not here yet—" he eyed the difficult
protestors, "I really want to think that you can
all hear and understand our point and will let
us keep the chickens. You don't know how
important they are to our family, to my daughter
especially..."

"You know, it really doesn't make much of
a point when everyone trying to convince us is in
your family. We know you're going to be bias." A
new voice said from the crowd.

"Well, um, does anyone volunteer? Anyone
have an opinion?"

"I do." Samson walked up. I wanted to hide.
But wait. The world slowed as I saw the oceans

in his eyes. He shook them away as he faced me and not the crowd, the put his normal face back on, the face that was angry. But I wouldn't forget the one that was just scared. "This chicken," he pointed directly at me, "viciously attacked me at school. That is why I decided to rally my friends and teachers to come here to protest the chickens. It is *justice* I value, and why should we let the tides of our hearts change our opinions? Just because they belong to a sad little girl who too unstable not to have tantrums at school means we should let our justice be inflicted? It's just ridiculous." He huffed, "What about if someone is a murderer but pretends to be all disabled?"

"Now there's a point." Someone agreed with the awful lies. I shuddered, and looked to Andrea, who was running to a woman I'd never seen before. Now she was talking to Andrea with that sad smile everyone I loved dearly had right now. I pulled my eyes off my girl and back to Samson, who was walking down from the steps. A stranger walked up.

"I am Johnny Pull, and my son Marcus goes to La Mesa Middle School and saw the chicken. I am on the City Council. I mostly agree with Samson. We can't give a leeway to anyone who just *wants* to break the law *really bad*. Whether or not they're "disabled". But beside this, I must say, this is not how petitions are supposed to work. It's so…different. Even if like, I mean, do any of you actually have a prepared, convincing speech or just random people from the crowd with loud opinions?"

"I have an opinion." Again Penny's voice tried to convince the people. "Andrea is different and so are her chickens, so I think it's fair that this group is too. If y'all just saw what it's like, if you really looked and let yourselves think…I mean and you put yourself in Andrea's place…" She tapered off, the crowd drowning her out again.

Then the woman who had been talking to Andrea walked up. "I am JoAnn Carol, and have been Andrea's speech therapist. I have not seen Andrea in several months, at which time she was almost completely non-verbal, and had a very difficult time dealing with emotions…"

"Get off the stairs! It's a stupid chicken! We don't want your sad little stories." The dejected woman walked down, and hugged Andrea, who was now crying. So was I. Then I saw Charlie next to me. He was holding the clipboard again. "Only 44 signatures. We need 200." He sighed.

Snowflake looked at me, fear overflowing from her bright blue eyes. **"We're not going home, Star. They're going to take us away forever!"**

"We can't give up, Snowflake, Lacey. We just can't. You…you know that." Was I telling them or myself? I wasn't sure.

I looked back at the stairs all the noise was silenced in my mind, I wasn't sure what to even think. It was Andrea was standing there.

Star
Chapter 24
Just Shine: 301

"Hello. My name is Andrea Johnson." I watched her flick her fingers twice, click her tongue once, and look from her own toes to just above and past the people's heads. And somehow her quiet voice drowned out the loud crowds.

"I know… you think my chickens should go away." She pronounced each word as if it were a precious jewel, and thought for long moments before they came all the way through. She paused often yet her point made it through, each moment a chance for the crowd to contemplate. "I really am sorry that they bother you." She flicked her fingers again. "I guess my chickens and I bother people a lot." My heart was pounding, and breaking and yet being made whole and new. Was she really doing this for us? "But please don't take them away. I…I know you don't…understand, and I don't understand…but…" She sighed and looked down again.

"You can do it, Andrea." I whispered, hoping my message would somehow reach her. She looked sideways to me, and a tiny smile crept up her lips before she continued.

"Maybe they are just animals. But…I mean…God, He can…He can use animals, and…and He has." She took a deep breath.

"These chickens have helped me more than anyone could realize. It's like I'm wearing a different shade of glasses, or like the world is kinda tilted differently to me, I guess, and... it can be confusing." She paused again for a very long time, and I was scared she was going to start crying, or just stop, but she started again. "My chickens have helped me learn, that different is okay. They're not dogs, they're chickens, but that's okay. And I'm not...not just "a girl with autism" I'm Andrea." She bit her lip, "I've never known how to understand people, and I still don't...but Star taught me...how to *love*. And, and it's better that understanding, it's...it's beyond that. And it...it makes me brave enough to try and get better, and, understand myself a little more, I suppose." Someone coughed and she jumped, but took in a breath and moved on. "I don't expect anyone to...understand, because...I can't understand. There's a wall between me and the world, but my chickens — Star, Lacey and Snowflake — " She let the names roll over her tongue, seeming to calm her slightly, and said it again, "Star, Lacey and Snowflake taught me that...that someone can love no matter who or what they are, or what they do. And that somehow God loves us no matter who we are, where we've been, or what we do. He loves all of you. And so should I, even if...if I'm different.

"So I'm just begging you, please, that you'd let my chickens stay, because you never know what other lessons we could learn. And…and if ever an animal earned their way to a heart, it was mine. And if they broke down the way to my heart," she looked up and right at all the people watching her, "maybe they can to yours, too." And she walked down, the crowd neither booing nor cheering, but sitting silently, so that a songbird was heard distantly chanting. And the silence dragged on, each second I was expecting some noise to shatter it and me with it, or to piece me back together. *Something.*

Then a bright haired and bright eyed girl bounded up the stairs. It was Penny. Her copper hair glittered as she took her stance.

"If…" She began uncertainly. Straightening up, she spoke louder. "If y'all can't listen to that, if you can't hear her humble, honest testimony, begging for grace, or justice or whatever you may believe it is, then…then you're about as blind as a rock and deaf as a tree. Andrea brought Star to school for *show and tell.* Lots of people bring animals for show and tell. People bring dogs and hamsters and things that you could just as well be allergic to. And could injure a kid more than a chicken. If…" she bit her lip, "I don't know what to say about it attacking Samson. I've been with the chickens time and time again and they've never been aggressive. Maybe…" She paused again, thinking before she spoke, "Maybe sometimes animals can see deeper into your heart than we let ourselves see? I know

137

that these birds love Andrea. And when I finally got to know her, (mostly because of the chickens, I might add) I finally saw what they saw: a girl who was just beautiful and amazing, and the most kind, precious person you ever saw, except you never saw it. You looked right past her. But the chickens didn't. They…I don't care if they're illegal or not. Livestock or small stock, does it really matter? I—" her voice broke suddenly, "I think that it should be enough to hear her story, of finding love, and her ability to tell us, when she's struggled with speaking for so long, as plenty enough to find some goodness, even when were all just masks over ourselves, to let the chickens stay. One small thing to help one another in this race of life. Of course we're all broken and we can't put this world back together, but it's the least we can do to restrain ourselves from pulling this little bit of it apart." She sighed, and walked down. And somehow the crowd no longer jeered and cried. Two girls with humble testimonies. And somehow their hearts began to melt, even if only a little. And then the miracle began taking shape.

Samson walked up again.

He was fidgety. Slowly clearing his throat and looked up through oceans.

"I—" He paused already, looking down at the ground for several seconds. "I am sorry." His voice was mumbled, and I was afraid I'd heard him wrong. "I'm so sorry." He said more loudly. "I—I really shouldn't have started this whole thing. We shouldn't …we shouldn't have be picking on Andrea just because of who she is. Maybe I shouldn't criticize everyone I meet and try to make their life awful just because mine has been." his voice broke and I saw his heart was breaking too. "I—I don't know what has happened to me in the past 30 minutes. I think we all build our own walls, maybe a little like Andrea's, to keep from being hurt, or being misunderstood or looking silly. And maybe, when that chicken chased me down the hall at school, she was trying to get through mine, enough to see again what life would be like without it. We forgot how to love. And somehow we were all just told that we are loved by the people who should hate us the most right now." He bit his lip and shrugged, like he was talking to just a classroom and not a whole crowd.

"So maybe this isn't supposed to be like this. Its all legal issues and that stuff that no body quite understands, but aren't personal stories better than that? I mean, Penny said it better than I could. Stories, *our stories* of love, loss, hope and healing, can't that be stronger than politics?" He looked at the ground. I was wrong, I guess maybe I just wanted to impress people or something, but I see that right now, I don't know what it is but there is something more to life than that. And, and I know that we shouldn't make those chickens go away. We just can't." He snatched the paper and jotted down his name. Then he handed it to the next person. "Pass this around. And if you agree with me, if you have any tenderness in your hearts, just sign your name. "

That was when people cheered. First a few timid claps, but it expanded in milliseconds, and it grew, until each individual clap turned into a loud, constant roar. Andrea covered her ears and ran to me. I tried to nuzzle her through the bars. Soon, however, it subsided, and the paper was given back to Charlie, and then given to member of the town council.

"Call a council meeting and decide now!" A voice called out.

"We can't just...I mean, it doesn't work like that...."

The calls persisted, and the flustered man shook his head frantically.

"Please." A girl tugged on his arm. It was Andrea. I hardly noticed she'd even left my side. "My chickens don't like being in little cages."

And not even the strongest of men and hardest of hearts could have refused her, I don't believe. And the meeting was arranged.

Time dragged on however, and Andrea sat and rubbed my waddles through the cage. Penny ran to Andrea and hugged her gently, then took each of her hands and smiled with happy and sad tears both in her eyes. "Andrea," she whispered, "Happy birthday."

Andrea smiled, "You figured it out?"

"301! It's the 301st day of the year. Andrea I'd do anything I can just to understand."

Andrea closed her eyes and leaned her head on Penny's shoulder. "You've done so much more than that." She sighed, "Thank you."

"Forever and always I would." Penny whispered as she sat with Lacey, rubbing her soft nape through the bars. Then Samson walked over nervously, scratching the back of his neck. "Can...can I see the chickens?" Andrea nodded and he sat down. Samson, *Samson* was scratching Snowflake, who flopped on her side like a dog allowing him to scratch her belly. No one said much for awhile, but finally the long silence was broken.

"I—I'm really sorry, both of you. I guess I never really knew how—how to...I have a hard time getting to know people, and like, being nice, ya know, and, no one has ever stuck around for me, and I guess you kinda showed me a little. My Grandma did too. But, I, I guess I wanna know if you can ever forgive me. I mean, I didn't understand you, Andrea, and like, I still don't, really. But that isn't an excuse for what I did. And I get that now. But, I, I've had people hurt me, too, and I don't want to be that kind of person. And I know it can be hard to, to see those people and not be mad and scared, so I can go away if you want." He sighed. "I'm rambling, I know."

"It's okay." Penny jumped in. "I...I forgive you. I'm not scared of you. We all build walls sometimes, and I won't hold any grudge. I can see you really mean it, and everyone can give a second chance."

He smiled a little. "Thank you. That, that really means a lot."

"'Forgive as you have been forgiven'" Andrea said. "I forgive you." And she smiled brightly.

"Samson," Penny whispered with a smirk, "it's Andrea's birthday."

He smiled. "Happy birthday Andrea!"

She shrugged "Thanks."

"Have you gotten any presents?"

Andrea frowned. "I just want my chickens."

And in that moment a loud clamor of people poured out of the town council hall.

Mr. Johnson was the one who walked over to the cages and his daughter. Samson and Penny stepped back shyly, but Mike kept Andrea from leaving. His face was not readable. He opened my cage and picked me up. He put me back where I belonged: in Andrea's arms. Then I saw his face was beaming, unable to contain his excitement, and I almost cackled from excitement. When his word came forth I couldn't hold it back.

"Andrea, your chickens are coming home. Your chickens who've changed lives."

And the cheer hit like a wave. Andrea and I hardly noticed this time, we were too busy enjoying each other's embrace. I loved her enough to let go, but holding on is so much better.

Chapter 25
Holding On: 320

The wind washed over my face with a sharp scent I'd never smelled before. A sound roared gently in my ears. My eyes met a vast expanse of surging blue. Then it hit me: it was the ocean. It was bigger than what I'd imagined in Andrea's eyes, and so, *so* beautiful, though scarcely more than hers. I looked up at Andrea from her arms. Her eyes were glued to the horizon, and they mirrored the very thing we walked towards. Gulls cried above out heads, the wind pushed Andrea's long hair, and the sound was silent under our feet. Finally, we reached the gentle ripple, and Andrea carefully put me down, holding onto my leash. I jumped a little as the cold liquid covered my feet.

"It's okay." Andrea said, bending over and stroking me. And it was. It felt…good. I looked up at Andrea, and she knelt down next to me.

"Together, we can face whatever oceans may come. Because I *like* the oceans now, Star. And me and you, in the palm of God's hand, we'll always keep our heads above water." She picked me up and looked into my eyes, "I don't know how to thank you. I don't know how to thank God for you. But this time, not knowing is just okay. No matter the oceans, I'll always have the tide of love. You really are my little Star." She smiled. A warm, beautiful splashing smile that was a thousand times more beautiful than the waves. She set me next to her mom on a picnic blanket, and ran, straight to the water, dancing and laughing in the waves, so different from that first time I'd seen her, silent and scared. I was so different, too. I watched her beautiful form and thought about it all. Lacey and Snowflake settled beside me on the blanket, Andrea in front of me, dancing, not fighting, the waves. Penny ran down and danced and laughed in the waves beside my Andrea. Samson was with his grandparents, he'd said they were going to adopt him, and they *would* stick around, he said, though it made fear flicker in his eyes when he said it. Mr. Johnson had gotten a job, and he started writing notes for Andrea every morning and she returned them each evening. Mrs. Johnson was next to me, watching her daughter,

understanding her a little better, and Andrea understanding her mom more too. A laugh was playing at her lips as she watched the girls.

And I thought about the people somewhere who didn't know. Who hadn't found themselves. Whose walls were still high and hard. It was still night after all. But we, *we* would be stars until the sun came one morning. No matter the way we talked, or how much we talked. If we were dogs, chickens, kids, adults, ASD or non-ASD, we could be stars.

We just had to take the love God, and with him, we would be stars and we would shine, together."   -Star

Epilogue

Penny and Andrea laughed as we all played, all of us. I smiled at my new friend, her silver stripes down her back like mine that faded what seemed like so long ago. She tumbled over her little yellow feet which were oversized for her small fuzzy body. Another yellow chick hopped over and pressed herself up against my feathers for snuggles. I preened her chick fuzz and smiled, **"Hey Kambii. You sleepy?"**

"Yeah," She yawned, **"and you're fuzzy."**

"Here, I've got an idea." Lacey said, leading the little Faverolle to Penny and sitting on her lap. **"Come here,"** And Kambii stumbled her way up Penny's lap, with a little help, and Lacey opened her wing, letting Kambii under, where the two snuggled, Penny stroking them both. Chickens were legal now, and Penny's parents let her get two little chicks. My mirror image strutted up to me, figuring out her feet at last. **"Hey Quetz."** I smiled, **"You sleepy too?"**

She giggled, **"Sleepy? No way! This yard you have, it's *huge!* I've only ever been in a little box. And it's *so small*. I want room like this!"** She spread out her little wings, just sprouting feathers. **"I want to explor— Aaa!"** A plane flew over dove under my wings.

"Hey, it's okay, Quetzalcoatl. It's just a plane."

"I wasn't *scared,* Star." She replied, hopping out into the open. I laughed, but decided not to argue.

It was she who turned to me curiously, **"I've heard from Penny a lot about you, and your person. Weren't you ever scared? I mean, how do you, like, when you were alone and weren't sure like even what it'd be like the next day! I...I want to be a chicken who isn't just a chicken, who's more than than, like you. But I don't know I can, I don't think I'm...really good enough, I guess."** She sighed and averted my gaze, preening her feathers absentmindedly, and nearly falling over in the process.

I used my beak to raise her face to mine, **"Quetzalcoatl—"**

"Don't call me by my *full name,* it's much too long."

I held back a laugh. **"Quetz, then, if all you ever do is love on Penny, sit with her when she needs you, sit on her shoulder, preen her hair, just love her you've done more amazing things than you can imagine. And even if you lose her, like I almost did, it makes it all worth it to know that you loved and gave her your all. You changed her life, and you'll change Kambii's too, just by loving them, Quetz. And...and there's no requirements to be worthy of loving."**

Quetz stood on her tippy toes and looked at me with her dark eyes, a smile growing on her face. **"We have a lot in common don't we?"**

I smiled and nudged her. "You bet we do, Quetz."

"I just hope I have a legacy like you do. My story to reach farther than a coop."

"It will Quetz, believe me, it already has."

Acknowledgements

I cannot thank everyone enough. First of all I thank my sister Annabel, the many late nights discussing the nuances and plot alterations, and staying a constant advisors as this story went from a simple sketch of an idea to the book, real book it is now. I thank my mom for listening to me ramble on about it, letting my voice my confusion in the publishing process and giving me the wisdom you have to push through and make it happen. And my dad for all of his publishing advice and leadership and design advice. I'd like to thank Grace, for never giving up on me and dealing with my seemingly insignificant questions like what bracelet Penny wears, I thank Zenia for hopping in halfway through the book but still giving me awesome input and letting me text her in the middle of the shutdown my questions, Madeline for just laughing at Snowflake with me, and clearing up so many mistakes too, Gracie, for supporting me even when she was away at school, Savannah encouraging me every step and being the one who introduced me to chickens in the first place years ago, Emily and Kaitlyn for also hopping in at the end and each of them all personally for just all the help and input you gave me being my beta readers and my writing club and supporting me as

I published it. Thank you to Mrs. Zinda for using a critical eye to help me make this story accurate as I learned about what autism is, and must admit I want to learn more about those who see through different lenses to the same world, and I have you to thank for opening that door for me. Thank you. Thank you so much to Bethany, Lilly, and Aunt Heather and for reading this in its stages and helping me work out any bumps, and being constant encouragement. Thank you to my grandparents for their constant support. Thank you to Marissa, Elise, Rachel, Nicole, Aubrey, Jordan, Leah, Grace and Sophia for your prayers as I wandered through the processes and listening to me ramble about my newest publication frustrations, it really means a ton. Thank you to Dave, you'll never read that I wrote this for you, but reading your books and knowing the testimony your life showed helped me so much through every step of this book, thank you. And thank You most of all to my Creator and Savior, who gave me the imagination to write this, who made any of it possible as He made me, and who gave me the strength to finish this work. Not to us, not to us, but to God be the glory.

-Molly Cox